THE SUTHERLIN FILES

DARK CURRENT RISING

ASHLEY FARLEY

Also By Ashley Farley

The Sutherlin Files

Dark Current Rising

Dark Current

Soul Seekers

Return to Marsh Hollow

Where Light lingers

When Sparks Fly

Cupid's Countdown

Messy Under the Mistletoe

The First Last Kiss

Sandy Island

Southern Discomfort

Beneath the Carolina Sun

Southern Simmer

Marsh Point

Long Journey Home

Echoes of the Past

Songbird's Second Chance

Heart of Lowcountry

After the Storm

Weekend on Sullivan's Island

Virginia Vineyards

Love Child

Blind Love

Forbidden Love

Love and War

Palmetto Island

Muddy Bottom

Change of Tides

Lowcountry on My Mind

Sail Away

Hope Springs Series

Dream Big, Stella!

Show Me the Way

Mistletoe and Wedding Bells

Matters of the Heart

Road to New Beginnings

Stand Alone

Scent of Magnolia

On My Terms

Tangled in Ivy

Lies that Bind

Life on Loan

Only One Life

Home for Wounded Hearts

Nell and Lady

Sweet Tea Tuesdays

Sweeney Sisters Series

Her Sisters Shoes

Lowcountry Stranger

Boots and Bedlam

Tangle of Strings

Saturdays at Sweeney's

Magnolia Series

Beyond the Garden

Magnolia Nights

Chapter One

I brace myself for impact. After weeks of tap dancing on a trapdoor, the hinges are ready to snap. A slap on the wrist would be generous. Getting pulled off the case is almost certain. I'll be lucky if I don't get fired. They don't hand out awards for the kind of messes I make.

I imagine all eyes on me as I push through the door of the station. Word travels fast, and Milo is the courier. He delivers his news with a smirk and a side of exaggeration—never missing a chance to make others look bad. And I have the dubious honor of being his favorite target.

I keep my head down as I make my way to the sergeant's office on the third floor. Morales is seated at his desk with his back to the door, typing away on his computer.

He barks at me without looking up. "Sit down, Sutherlin."

"Yes, sir." I drop into the chair opposite his desk, waiting while he finishes whatever urgent business keeps his fingers flying.

Finally, he spins around, his face softening when he sees me. "You look tired."

I huff out a laugh. "You have four grown daughters. You should know better than to tell a woman she looks tired."

He presses his lips into a thin line as my attempt at a joke crashes and burns. "I speak only the truth, Sutherlin."

My shoulders sag with the breath I've been holding all afternoon. "About today, sir. I can explain. The officers assured us the scene was secure. When I heard a noise in the closet, I assumed it was our suspect. I wasn't expecting a kid."

Morales studies me, his expression unreadable. "I've been briefed on the situation. You drew your gun on a child and froze." His voice remains calm, but his words hit like a fist. "But this isn't just about today, Sutherlin. You haven't been yourself lately. Understandably so—you've been through a lot."

"I'm fine, Sarge. People get divorced every day."

"Not like this. Grayson humiliated you in front of the whole city—tossed you out like yesterday's trash and left you with nothing."

Heat creeps up my neck. "Well, when you put it like that."

"I don't mean to be so hard on you, but you know I'm right."

I *do* know he's right, much as admitting it kills me. My husband made a laughingstock of me. Stomped on my pride, wrung me out, and hung me up for the neighbors to gawk at. If humiliation were an Olympic sport, Grayson would've taken home the gold.

Morales curls his fingers around the edge of the desk, bracing himself. Here comes the hammer. "You need time, Lane, to get your head on straight."

"With all due respect, sir, what I need is to see this case through. We're closer than we've ever been to putting Virelli in cuffs. An eyewitness placed him at the scene and confirmed he took a round in today's shootout. We've issued an APB, and every unit is on the lookout."

Morales shakes his head. "I'm sorry, Sutherlin. I can't overlook what happened today."

My eyes squeeze shut as the scene slams back into me—blood on the floor, the woman's body, noise behind the closet door, terrified toddler crouching in the corner. I hear the sound so clearly now, a soft whimpering. How did I mistake a person in distress for danger?

I blink the memory away. Morales is still watching me, his expression twisted in a mix of pity and sympathy. "I'm giving you thirty days. Paid. You need to rest. Grieve. Put some distance between yourself and everything that's been eating at you. I'm not firing you, Lane—I'm trying to save you."

"But, sir. I—"

His hand shoots up, silencing me. "No argument. Get out of town for a while. Go home to Tidewell! Let Hollis feed you for a few days. You could stand to put on some weight." He opens the bottom drawer of his desk and sets a small lockbox on top. "You know the drill."

"Yes, sir." I unclip my badge and set it gently beside the box. The gun takes longer. I hold on to it an extra beat before finally placing it inside.

"It's just temporary, Sutherlin."

"Right. Just temporary." I stand abruptly and hurry out of the station—eyes on the floor as I fight back my emotions. Crying doesn't cut it in this line of work.

I'm almost to my Bronco when Amanda catches up. "Hey, Lane. We're going to happy hour. Wanna come?" Her smile fades when she sees my face. "Oh, honey. I'm so sorry. I heard about today. You look like you could use a drink."

I picture the other detectives crammed around a sticky table, beer sloshing from pitchers as they pick apart the shootout in gory detail. "Thanks, but I need to clear my head. I'm going home for a run."

I slide into the driver's seat and shut the door, blocking out the world with a hollow thud. In five o'clock traffic, it takes me thirty minutes to crawl three miles to what passes for home—a cramped one-bedroom in a rundown brick building on the Boulevard. Not exactly the kind of place you bring company, but it's close to Byrd Park, and I need somewhere to run.

I'd donated my thrift-store finds and hand-me-down furniture when I moved in with Grayson. None of it belonged in his sleek Monument Avenue condo. Turns out, neither did I. But when he tossed me out, I left with only the clothes on my back—not even the antique mirror he gave me for my birthday.

The décor here redefines minimalist. A lone barstool holds down the breakfast counter, while a threadbare Goodwill sofa sags in the living room. The bedroom isn't much better—a queen mattress jammed into the space with a plastic crate pulling duty as a nightstand. No dresser, only neat stacks of clothes lined up on the floor by the closet.

Maybe I'll use this thirty-day exile to spruce the place up. Or at least buy a second barstool so it looks like I have friends.

I change into running clothes, cinch my laces, and bolt out the door. At Byrd Park, I push harder with each lap around Boat Lake, pounding the path until the world blurs and my lungs burn. Still, Morales's words chase me, dogging every stride. *I'm not firing you, Lane—I'm trying to save you.*

While it isn't officially a suspension, it feels like exile—like being benched in the playoffs with the game on the line. How can he pull me now? For six months I've been building evidence against Nico Virelli, the most ruthless gang leader I've ever gone up against. He's finally in my grasp. We're so damn close. And I blew it.

I see it again—sharper this time. My gun up. Closet door kicked wide. Finger tight on the trigger.

And there he is. A toddler. No more than three. Tear-streaked cheeks. Little fists balled like he's ready to fight the world.

Milo's voice echoes, muffled, like it's coming from underwater. "What're you doing, Sutherlin? It's a kid. Put your gun down."

I freeze. Paralyzed.

"Detective! Lower your weapon. Now!" Milo again, sharper this time, cutting through the fog.

My hands shake as I shove the gun back into its holster and scoop the boy into my arms. His mama's body lies in the next room. His daddy—if he survives his wounds—will end up in prison for a very long time.

This little boy's life shattered in an instant. He'll grow up too fast now, bounced to a grandmother or maybe an aunt. Either way, he deserves more than the wreckage left behind.

Up ahead, a cyclist barrels around the bend, nearly plowing into me, snapping me back to the present. I stumble to a stop, bent double, hands braced on my knees, breath sawing in and out. When the last of my strength gives out, I sink onto a patch of grass and bury my face in my palms as the dam finally breaks.

I can't remember the last time I cried—not since before Grayson's affair. I've been holding it all in—the sadness, the fury, the crushing sense of failure. And it has almost cost me my job. Damn Grayson.

I fall back in the grass, forearm draped over my eyes. No one bothers to stop. No one cares about a woman writhing on the ground, ugly crying in the open.

By the time I push myself upright, the tears have left me hollow, not healed. My throat is raw, my chest tight, like I've carved something out but left the wound wide open. Maybe crying isn't weakness. But it sure as hell isn't strength either. It's survival—barely.

I imagine Morales's face if I showed up tomorrow, all better because I had a good cry. A harsh laugh escapes. As if it were that easy.

I brush the grass off my shorts, draw in a shaky breath, and force my chin up as I retrace my steps around the lake. The early September air carries the faintest hint of fall, a reminder the world keeps moving whether or not I'm ready.

Maybe Morales was right. Maybe I should go home. I haven't set foot in Tidewell in nearly two years—not for a quick visit, not even for my father's retirement party. I've been dodging the one conversation I can't avoid forever. The divorce.

My father—Judge Hollis Sutherlin—will always be *Your Honor* back home. Revered across the Commonwealth, courted by politicians, sought by preachers. When I married Grayson—an ambitious young attorney—Dad puffed out his chest with pride. The old-school Southern judge took the up-and-coming criminal attorney under his wing, grooming him for greatness.

So how will he react when he learns Grayson tossed me aside for someone younger? That his handpicked protégé humiliated his daughter in front of the whole damn city.

Dad always hoped one of his children would follow in his footsteps and become a lawyer. When that didn't happen, his only daughter marrying a criminal attorney was, in his eyes, the next best thing. The disappointment I will surely find in his eyes is why I've put off breaking the news.

Still, the thought of home tugs at something soft in me—curling up on the porch swing, watching the sun sink behind the trees, eating my daddy's crispy hushpuppies and creamy cheese grits.

But I'm done running. I won't hide behind Dad's mahogany desk. Not this time. I refuse to let Grayson's betrayal be the thing that breaks me. I'll stay in Richmond, walk into Morales's office tomorrow, and ask for another shot. I *have* to stay on the Virelli case. I've worked too hard to let it slip away now.

Twenty minutes later, as I'm stepping out of the shower, my phone buzzes against the sink counter. A text from Amanda—a group selfie from happy hour. Milo is front and center, wearing that smug expression he's perfected.

Another message follows.

Come join us! It's not the same without you.

I power off my phone before they blow it up.

Dinner is a bowl of cereal eaten over the sink, the apartment silent except for the hum of the fridge. I fall into bed early, too drained to do anything else, and sleep pulls me under like a dark tide.

Morning comes too soon. I drag myself to the kitchen and start the coffee, finally turning my phone back on while the stream of brew drips into the pot. A flood of unread messages lights up the screen. My heart skips a beat as I click on the one that matters most. Why is Dad texting me in the middle of the night?

> Morning, Laney Bug. I hate to be the bearer of bad news, but I wanted you to hear it from me. Addie's missing. She took Scout for a walk after dinner yesterday and never came back.

Panic grips my chest as I scroll through the rest of my messages. All from coworkers. Nothing about Addie.

I switch to my phone app, and my finger freezes over the missed call. A voicemail. From Addie.

I hit play.

Her voice bursts through, trembling, breathless. *"Laney! I need your help. I've gotten myself into trouble. I don't—"*

The message cuts out.

Chapter Two

"Addie! Addie!" I shout into the phone like she can hear me, like the sound of my voice might bring her back.

My hands shake as I stab at her number. One ring. Two. Three. Four—and voicemail. I hang up and hit redial. Damn! Voicemail again. This time I leave a message, my voice ragged. "Addie, please. Are you okay? Call me back. I'm worried sick."

I drop onto the barstool and share Addie's voicemail to Voice Memos. Opening the file, I drag the playback speed down, listening for anything I might've missed. Addie doesn't just sound breathless and panicked. She sounds terrified. And beneath her voice, there's a noise. Faint. Familiar. It prickles my skin and makes the hair on the back of my neck stand on end. Is that the rumble of a car engine approaching?

I drum my fingers on the counter, my brain too rattled to think clearly. There must be a way to connect with her. I open the Find My app, praying for the familiar blinking dot. Instead, the screen flashes back a message I've never seen for Addie. *Location not available.* My stomach knots. Addie would never turn off location sharing—she's meticulous about safety. Which means her phone is off. Or dead. Or smashed to pieces at the bottom of Oyster Bay.

The thought slams into me like a gut punch.

I glance down at the call log. The message came in at 9:42 p.m. If she walked the dog after supper—say, seven o'clock—where was she in those missing two hours?

I scroll through my contacts and tap Josh in Tech Ops. He answers on the third ring.

"I need a favor," I blurt.

He grunts. "Good morning to you too."

"Sorry. Morning. I need a favor." I'm pacing now. "Can you pull the tower hit from a call? Number's down in Tidewell."

The pause stretches long enough that I know what's coming. When he speaks again, his voice has shifted—careful, suspicious. "Tidewell? As in the Northern Neck? You got a warrant, Lane?"

"No time for warrants." My voice tightens. "The phone belongs to my best friend. She left me a voicemail around nine thirty. She was out of breath, like she'd been running, and she sounded terrified. My dad texted me around one thirty—she's missing. I just need the tower hit from her call. A place to start. That's it."

Silence. I can hear him weighing the risks. I soften the edge in my voice. "Please, Josh. I've known Addie since kindergarten. She's family. And she's missing."

Another beat. "Something's wrong, Josh. I can feel it."

Finally, he sighs. "All right. But this is gray-area stuff, Lane. I'll see if I can pull the CDR. Text me the number—and don't make this a habit."

"Thank you, Josh. I owe you one."

I forward Addie's contact and jump to my feet. Time to pack.

Halfway to the bedroom, I freeze. What about my job? What about the Virelli case? Should I really drop everything and run down to Tidewell? Addie could walk through her front door any minute with a perfectly logical explanation.

But what if she doesn't? This is Addie. *My* Addie.

Today is Friday. I'll spend the weekend in Tidewell—figuring out what's going on with Addie and breaking the news to Dad about my divorce. I'll be back in time for work on Monday.

Morales will assume I took the weekend to rest and clear my head. Then he'll put me back on the case where I belong.

I stuff toiletries and several changes of clothes into a duffel bag, then hesitate at the bedroom closet. Something's missing. I snap my fingers. Right. I turned in my badge and gun to Morales. I lift the mattress and pull my personal Glock from its case, thumb the safety, check my concealed-carry permit in my wallet, and lock the apartment behind me.

I call my dad as I'm driving through town. He answers in that clipped, no-nonsense tone he uses with everyone but me. "Hollis Sutherlin."

The sound of his voice twists something in my gut—everything I've been avoiding. Tidewell. The divorce. His disappointment.

"Hey, Dad. It's me. Have you heard anything more about Addie's disappearance?"

Silence.

"Dad? Are you there?"

"Oh. Lane. It's you. No, I haven't heard anything."

"How'd you find out she was missing?"

"Franklin told me. He had a few deputies searching the area around midnight. Woke me up banging on the door, asking if I'd seen or heard anything."

Franklin Boone is the Tidewell sheriff—and my father's longtime friend. Boone has been in and out of my life for as long as I can remember—the kind of man who thinks every problem can be solved with a firm handshake and a Bible verse. Of course he'd start his search in Founders State Park. Addie often runs the winding trails that back up to our property, River Birch Farm.

I flip on my blinker, cut across traffic, and take the exit onto Highway 64. "Addie usually runs in the park in the morning. Your message said she was walking the dog after supper yesterday evening. I doubt she'd go to the park after dark."

"My message?" Confusion edges his voice.

I let out a dry chuckle. Typical Dad—probably lost in a crossword puzzle from today's paper. "Check your phone. You texted me late last night. Anyway, I'm on my way home now. I hope you don't mind me bunking with you this weekend."

"Of course not, Bug. I look forward to seeing you."

"Me too. In the meantime, let me know if you hear anything more about Addie."

"Will do. Drive safely, Elaine."

I drop the phone into the cupholder. *Elaine?* Dad hasn't called me by my given name since… since never. Was he just distracted? Or hiding something? Does he know more about Addie's disappearance than he's letting on?

I shove the thought aside. He wouldn't do that. Dad doesn't keep things from me.

I set my cruise control, avoiding the urge to speed, and let my thoughts drift to Addie. Truth be told, I'm surprised she called me at all. We haven't spoken since Christmas before last—no, Thanksgiving, when Grayson and I came home for the family reunion. Back when everything in my world still felt right.

Add Addie to the list of people I haven't told about my divorce. She wouldn't understand. She's blissfully married to the town heartthrob—the deputy every lonely housewife flirts with while reporting suspicious noises and missing porch packages. To Addie, marriage is sacred, no matter the cost. Which is why it makes no sense she would vanish on Clay like this.

There has to be a simple explanation. Maybe she stopped by her mom's house and fell asleep on the couch. She's close to Mama Jean—visits her all the time. Surely, this is a misunderstanding.

But then why call me? Why did she sound so scared?

The investigator in me knows this doesn't look good. I need to act like a detective, not a best friend.

The miles blur, my mind chasing itself in circles—Addie's panicked voice, Dad calling me Elaine, Morales's warning for me to get some rest. By the time I turn off the main highway toward Tidewell, my chest is as tight as a noose drawn one notch too close. Home has always been equal parts comfort and chokehold. I want to believe Addie's okay, that this trip is just a false alarm. But the pressure only builds as I cross the bridge into town.

I'm waiting at the main intersection on Tidewater Drive when Josh calls. "Your friend's phone last pinged Tower 337A—just off Tidewater Drive near Patriots Landing Marina."

My grip tightens on the wheel. "Patriots Landing? Are you sure it wasn't closer to Founders Park? That's where she usually runs."

"I don't know Tidewell, Lane. I'm just reading the map. Tower 337A, around 9:30 p.m." His voice drops. "Listen . . . word's getting around about your leave of absence. People are speculating it's more than burnout. You know how it is—whispers, assumptions. I'm not supposed to be doing this, so keep it between us."

Whispers? Assumptions? Josh is being kind. I'm sure the talk is worse—especially if Milo's behind it.

"I'll never tell a soul. I promise," I manage, choking out the words before ending the call.

I sit in a daze, thumbs drumming the steering wheel. None of this makes any sense. The light turns green, but I don't move until a horn blares behind me.

Instead of turning left onto Tidewater Drive toward home, I wrench the wheel right toward the historic waterfront. Tidewell's tidy row of shops and clapboard cafes streaks past my window— antique signage, fresh paint, tourists strolling with shopping bags. It all feels strangely unreal, like I've slipped into someone else's life.

I follow Route 22 for two more miles until the bustle of town gives way to the salt-stained quiet of Patriots Landing Marina. The Pearl at Oyster Bay, Tidewell's boutique resort, looms just beyond—its crisp white façade and manicured palms a stark contrast to the rougher charm of the docks.

The cell tower covers too much ground—like looking for a shell in a sandstorm. There are at least a hundred boats here—

sleek sailboats, gleaming motor yachts, a few tired old fishing rigs with more rust than hull. Addie could be on any of them. Or none at all.

I'd need a team to canvass the area, which means calling the sheriff's office. Despite being Dad's best friend, Sheriff Boone and I have history—unfinished business I'm not interested in revisiting.

My stomach growls, reminding me I haven't eaten all morning. I can't remember my last real meal. Cereal for dinner last night hardly counts. I lick my lips, thinking about Dad's famous omelets. Food will help me recharge.

Circling the marina lot, I head back toward town. I've only gone a quarter mile when a faded sign catches my eye. *Bayview Refuse Center*—better known around here as the Bayview dump.

Something pulls me in—a hunch I can't ignore. I can't imagine Addie walking Scout down this lonely stretch after dark, but her phone pinged a tower near here, and my gut says look.

I ease onto Bayview Drive and slow to a crawl, headlights sweeping over a wall of pine trees lining the road. The forest presses close, shadows tangled and deep, the kind of place that swallows light. I picture it at night—black as pitch, branches clawing the sky—and a shiver snakes up my spine.

Three hundred feet past the dump's entrance, something catches my eye. A pale heap by the marshy shoulder, crumpled against the grass. My heart leaps. *Please don't let it be Addie.*

I pull up beside the shape and let out a shaky breath. Not a body. A dog.

Scout?

I slam the Bronco into park and step out, moving slowly. The closer I get, the surer I am—Addie's yellow lab, unmistakable with that wavy mohawk of fur running down her back.

"Hey, girl," I murmur, kneeling beside the shivering dog. "Remember me? I haven't seen you in a minute."

Her fur gleams golden, like Addie's thick hair. *Our golden girl,* we used to call her back in high school—all-state in swimming, all-American in lacrosse, salutatorian of our graduating class.

I stroke Scout's head. Her coat is damp, paws caked with mud. Why the mud? Was she in the marsh? Is Addie still in there? Did something happen here?

I press my nose to Scout's neck, breathing in the wet-dog smell. "Don't worry. I'll find her. I'll bring your mama back to you. I promise."

Straightening, I pull out my phone and call the sheriff's office.

"Tidewell Sheriff's Office," a woman answers, voice flat with boredom.

"I need to speak to Sheriff Boone."

"He's not here right now," she says. "He's out on a big case. Missing young woman, in case you haven't heard."

"I heard," I snap. "Patch me through to him."

"I'm sorry, ma'am. I can't do that."

"This is Detective Lane Sutherlin, Richmond PD. Put me through to him. Now!"

A beat of silence, then her tone shifts. "Right away, ma'am. Hold the line."

I hear a click, followed by the sound of ringing, then Boone's deep voice. "Lane? That you?"

"Yes, sir. I found Addie's dog—on Bayview Drive, just past the dump."

"Don't move. I'm on my way. Be there in five."

In Tidewell, everything's five minutes away.

I grab an old blanket from the Bronco, drape it over the trembling dog, and settle beside her to wait.

True to his word, Boone's cruiser rolls up in under five. I stand, brushing dirt from my jeans. He climbs out, tips his hat. "Well, I'll be damned. Good to see you, Lane. You're looking . . ." His eyes sweep over me. "Skinny."

I arch a brow. "That's one way to say hello. Nice to see your manners haven't changed."

"No doubt you heard about Addie from Hollis. I figured you'd come running." He scratches Scout behind her ears. "So . . . what's going on here? Lucky guess? Or were you dropping off trash and stumbled upon the dog?"

"Neither. She called me last night."

Boone's expression hardens. "Addie did?"

I nod. "She didn't say much. Just that she needed my help. Then the line went dead."

Boone rubs his stubble, eyes narrowing. "And you didn't think to notify me?"

"I contacted a friend at Richmond PD," I say evenly. "He pulled the tower records. Showed her phone near the marina, so I drove by. Something told me to check this road."

"Mm-hmm." He throws his shoulders back, his belly pressing against the buttons of his khaki uniform. "Why'd you call me instead of Clay? You're Addie's best friend. He's her husband."

"Protocol, sir," I say, shifting my gaze away.

Boone grunts, pulling out his phone. He taps the screen with a thick finger. The ringing blares through his speaker, and then Clay's voice cuts in, sharp with nerves. "What is it, Sheriff? Did you find her?"

"Not yet. But Lane found her dog out by the Bayview dump. I'm with her now. You're on speaker." He gives a quick rundown—Addie's call to me last night, the Patriots Landing tower hit.

"Any sign of my wife?" Clay asks.

"Nope," I say—my first words to him. "Do you want me to bring Scout to you?"

He doesn't hesitate. "I can't deal with a high-energy dog right now. Can you keep her?"

I lock eyes with Boone, biting back my irritation. He wants me —a virtual stranger to the dog—to keep her when her mom is missing, when she's already shaken and confused. Scout deserves comfort, not another disruption. But I swallow the words. The man's wife is missing, after all.

"I guess."

"Good. I'll leave her food and some of her things on the front porch."

Typical Clay. Always expecting the world to bow down to him.

I open the back door of the Bronco and call for Scout. The dog leaps in, then scrambles into the front passenger seat.

I can't help but smile. "I see. So that's how it is. Might be nice to have a four-legged friend riding shotgun for a while."

I pull away from the marsh and head for River Birch Farm—hoping the old place will offer a moment's peace . . . and maybe a little clarity.

Chapter Three

The river birch trees lining the long drive spread their arms wide, welcoming me home, their pale bark curling like parchment in the early-afternoon light. Dad planted them after Tommy died nineteen years ago—a living memorial to a life cut short and a quiet reminder that grief, given enough time, can grow into something beautiful.

My family's historic home comes into view, nestled at the end of the gravel lane like an old friend waiting on the porch. Built before the Civil War and purchased by my grandparents in the 1920s, the weathered farmhouse has been expanded and modernized many times, but it still clings stubbornly to the charm of the original structure.

I park in the circular drive behind Dad's early nineties Wagoneer and wander around the front yard while Scout does her business. At first glance, everything looks in order—shrubs trimmed, fescue grass free of weeds, shutters still tight against the house. But then I notice the paint peeling under the eaves, a gutter sagging at one corner, a split rung on the porch railing. Dad would never have allowed such lapses before. Is he no longer spending his weekends with hammer in hand?

I cross the porch and open the heavy mahogany door. Inside, a wide center hallway anchors the house, with rooms branching off like spokes on a wheel—formal dining and living rooms to the right, my father's paneled study and the family library to the left, its shelves lined with first editions and signed copies collected over generations. Straight ahead, a curving staircase—grand enough for Scarlett O'Hara—sweeps up to the second floor.

I move through the hallway into the family room, where most of our lives play out—lounging, eating, the TV always humming in the background. Double doors open onto a wide porch that stretches the length of the house. Steps drop to a terraced patio, and beyond it, Oyster Creek unfurls in a broad sweep of water and sky.

Dad stands at the counter in the adjacent kitchen, slathering Duke's mayo on two slices of white bread. He looks up from his task, surprise etched across his face.

"Oh. Hey, Lane. I wasn't expecting you."

I frown. "What do you mean? I told you I was coming when we spoke earlier."

His eyes cloud for a beat. "Right. I just thought you'd be here later," he says, like he's trying to plaster over a blank spot.

So he wasn't just distracted earlier. Something's going on with him—and it has nothing to do with Addie's disappearance. I have a dozen questions, but I just got here. Probably not the best time to launch a full cross-examination.

His gaze drops to the dog wagging its tail at my side. "When'd you get a dog?"

"It's Addie's dog, Scout. I'm keeping her for Clay until we find Addie." Rounding the counter, I find a bowl and fill it with water. As she laps it up, I can't help but wonder when she last ate or drank—and what she might've witnessed in the past twelve hours. If only dogs could talk. Or testify.

"Are you hungry?" Hollis asks.

"Starving. I've been craving one of your omelets since I left Richmond this morning—goat cheese, caramelized onions, spinach, chives. I'll get everything ready." I open the refrigerator and pause, the little hairs at the back of my neck prickling. The shelves are nearly empty—no milk, no cheese, not even a carton of eggs. My gourmet dad usually keeps it stocked with all manner of delectable things.

"Dad?" I ask slowly. "When's the last time you went to the grocery store?"

He waves me off with the butter knife. "A couple of days ago. I don't keep much food in the house anymore. No one here but me."

What? No company? He usually has a revolving door of visitors, especially on the weekends—old friends, associates, lawyers, and judges from across the Commonwealth.

I shut the refrigerator. "I have to run back to town later for some of Scout's things. I'll stop by the market while I'm out."

"Would you like a sandwich?" Hollis asks.

I glance down at the package of dried-up ham. "Tempting, but no. I'll grab something in town."

"Suit yourself."

I lean against the counter, watching Dad slap the thin slices of ham onto bread with none of the care he once gave to plating a gourmet meal. This is the same man who used to turn this kitchen into a stage—whisk in hand, music playing, aromas curling through the air. Now he's settling for a tired ham sandwich. He's aged in the nearly two years since I was last home— hair mostly gray, crow's feet etched deeper. The sharp-eyed judge, who once ruled a courtroom with an iron gavel, has been replaced by a man whose shoulders are sagging under the weight of time.

"How's your husband? He didn't come with you?" Hollis asks, cutting his sandwich in half.

My husband? Does he not remember his name? "Let's wait and talk about Grayson over dinner. What would you like to cook? Should I pick up some fish from the seafood market?"

"Sure," he says, lifting a shoulder in a half shrug.

Is that shoulder bonier than usual? Has he lost weight? Hard to tell in his lounge pants and sweatshirt. And when did he stop wearing khakis and a button-down?

I straighten, forcing the concern down. "All right, then. I'll unpack, then head back to town."

"Why don't you stay in the cottage?" Hollis says around a bite of sandwich.

Surprise flashes through me. "Are you serious?" The little yellow cottage down by the water has always been reserved for his out-of-town guests—off limits to everyone else.

"Sure, why not? I'm not expecting company. You'll have more privacy out there, and you'll need the extra room for the dog."

"The cottage sounds great, Dad. Thanks," I say, heading toward the mudroom.

I'm almost at the back door when he calls after me, "Be sure to clean up after his mess."

"*Her* mess, Dad," I holler back. "Scout's a she."

I drive the short distance down the hill to the waterfront. The cottage smells faintly of must and salt air, but otherwise, everything appears in order. Lally—our family's longtime housekeeper —keeps the place clean and ready for unexpected guests. How long has it been since any actually came?

Choosing the larger of the two bedrooms, I unpack my bag and open the sliding doors. Stepping onto the small porch, I breathe in the briny scent of Oyster Creek. The sky is a soft periwinkle, the water rippling under a gentle breeze.

Somewhere out there, Addie is missing. Statistically, the odds of finding her alive shrink with each passing hour. The detective in me imagines the worst, and a shiver racks my body as I picture her drifting beneath the surface.

I turn my back on the creek. Every second counts. So what next? I need to talk to Addie's family and friends to get a clearer timeline.

I tuck my pistol into the waistband at my hip, grab my keys, and head for the door. Scout trots after me, nails clicking on the wood floor. I hesitate—I could take her. With the windows cracked, she'd be fine while I run into the market. But pulling up to Addie's house and her not being there might be more unsettling for Scout. Best to leave her here. After all, she's had a traumatic night, abandoned in the marsh in the pitch-black dark. She could use a rest.

I pat Scout's head. "Stay here, girl. I won't be long."

I drive back up the hill, gravel crunching under the tires, the creek glittering in my rearview mirror. Addie and I used to string crab off the dock, our laughter echoing off the trees. By tomorrow, they might be dragging these waters for her body.

Chapter Four

Addie and Clay live in a row of old houses on the historic side of the bridge, their weathered clapboards painted in soft coastal hues—seafoam green, butter yellow, oyster white. Most have been lovingly updated, with tidy front yards edged in picket fences and window boxes spilling over with geraniums and trailing ivy. Clay and Addie's place is no exception, with its wide porch lined with rocking chairs and a faded American flag that flutters in the breeze, worn thin from too many Fourth of July barbecues.

As I approach the porch, I catch the muffled thump of bass from inside—Jimmy Buffett, an interesting choice for a man whose wife is missing. Waiting on the top step is an assortment of dog bowls, beds, and worn collars—everything but food. Just the excuse I need to talk to Clay.

I press the doorbell and wait. And wait. When he doesn't answer, I pound my fist on the door. I'm rewarded by the sound of quick footsteps and a rattling doorknob.

Clay appears in the doorway wearing only a towel slung low around his waist, his damp hair sticking up in wild tufts—more of Clay Dalton than I ever wanted to see. He's the kind of man who spends more time in the mirror than on his marriage. Not my type —not even on a very lonely night with bad lighting.

Breathless, Clay grips the doorframe, gulping air. "Geez, Lane. What's with the banging? Please tell me you've got news about Addie."

"Sorry. I don't. I came for Scout's things. You forgot to leave me any food."

Is that relief or disappointment flickering across his face? Hard to tell. "Hang on a sec." He shuts the door without inviting me inside.

Five minutes later, he reappears in khaki shorts and a blue striped golf shirt. Flung over his shoulder is a large bag of dog food —not a small container. He's planning for Scout to stay awhile.

"Here. Let me put this in your car." Brushing past me, he hefts the bag into the back of the Bronco and drops the hatch with a solid thunk.

Turning toward me, he shields his eyes from the sun, voice casual like we'd just bumped carts in the frozen food aisle. "So . . . how long are you staying in town?"

"Until I find Addie," I deadpan.

"Are you officially on the case?"

"Nope. This isn't my jurisdiction. But I will find her. Where were you last night?"

He rocks back on his heels, arms folding loose . . . too loose. "Since you're not officially working the case, I don't have to answer that."

"Correct. But you look suspicious if you don't."

He rolls his eyes. "Whatever. I have nothing to hide. After we ate supper, Addie took Scout for a walk, and I—"

"What time was that?" I cut in, pulling up the Notes app on my phone.

"A few minutes after seven. I went out to the shed to clean my guns—getting ready for hunting season. I finished around nine. When I came back to the house, she still wasn't home."

"What then?"

"Drove around looking for her. Checked the park. Called a few people—Trina, Mama Jean. Around eleven, I gave up and called the sheriff."

I make a mental note to confirm the timestamp on that call.

"Anything else I should know?" I ask, thumbs tapping the screen.

His face stays neutral, but the corners of his mouth twitch like he's chewing on something bitter. "She's always wearing those skimpy exercise clothes, even when she's just walking the dog. I warned her she was asking for trouble."

The comment makes my jaw tighten. Blaming Addie is a cheap shot—like she brought whatever happened to her on herself. "Do you remember what kind of *skimpy clothes* she had on last night?" I ask, unable to keep the sarcastic edge out of my tone.

He grimaces as though the memory physically pains him. "How could I forget? Pink sports bra, gray running shorts cut high, bare stomach. Some sick bastard probably snatched her." He lowers his head, swiping at his eyes. "She's long gone by now."

"Why are you so sure she's gone?" Before he can respond, I slide into the Bronco. Through the windshield, as I back out of the driveway, I see him still standing there, mouth half open like a caught fish.

I cross over the bridge to the new section of town where everything oversized has staked its claim—McMansions with six-car garages, mega-churches with parking lots the size of football fields, and law offices masquerading as antebellum estates. Hard to believe this stretch used to be soybean fields and scrub pine, back when Tidewell still felt small. Now, a massive shopping center boasts a Target, Chick-fil-A, and Publix—the Holy Trinity of suburban commerce.

At Publix, I load up a cart with some of Dad's favorites along with a few of my own—yogurt, granola, bananas. I've just rounded the aisle toward the produce section when I spot the Bramble twins. Ducking my head, I pivot toward the coffee display on the endcap, grateful for the shadow of my baseball hat.

Luanne and Susanne—nicknamed Lulu and Suzy—haven't been separated since birth. They even married brothers. And even though they're thirty-five years old, they still dress alike—sorta. Today they're both wearing jeans and pink tops with their auburn hair pulled back in matching ponytails. The sound of their voices is the only way I can tell them apart. Lulu's is high and squeaky, while Suzy's is deep—like Suzy got too much of the voice gene and Lulu not nearly enough.

"I hear Lane's back in town," Lulu squeaks, sniffing the stem end of a cantaloupe.

Her twin bobs her head. "Yep! Big city detective flew in on her broom to rescue Addie from the monster who kidnapped her."

Lulu drops the melon into her cart. "I still don't get how those two are friends. Addie has everything going for her—looks, brains, charm—and Lane is her dark shadow."

That's me—the strange girl no one ever understood. Tidewell folks love their roles—the golden boy, the hometown sweetheart, the screwup. I drew the weirdo card. Richmond might be messy, but at least nobody cares enough to stick me with a label.

"Shame on Lane for not coming sooner," Lulu adds. "What with poor Judge Sutherlin's diagnosis and all."

My ears perk up. Diagnosis? What diagnosis? I risk a glance in their direction. Suzy's eyes are narrowed, as though this might be news to her too.

"Careful what you say, Lulu," her twin murmurs. "His disease hasn't been confirmed yet."

"So? It's only a matter of time. Everyone knows he has Alzheimer's." Lulu pushes her cart toward the bagged salad section, Suzy trailing behind.

I watch them go. Tidewell's own version of breaking news—served up in the produce aisle by the Bramble twins, who've never let facts get in the way of a good rumor. Same old story—heavy on drama, light on truth.

On the drive back to River Birch, the twins' gossip clings to me like the chill from the produce aisle, but it's what happened earlier in the kitchen that keeps looping in my head. Dad forgetting I was coming. The empty refrigerator. The Hollis Sutherlin I know doesn't *forget* groceries. He plans menus, stocks the fridge like a chef prepping for a banquet.

It could be nothing, I tell myself. People his age slow down. They forget. They eat simpler. But then I remember his sudden, unexpected retirement a year ago. He claimed he wanted more time for fishing and odd jobs around the house. At the time, I was too tangled in my own mess to question it.

Now, I can't shake the image of him in that faded sweatshirt, slapping dried-up ham between two slices of bread. It feels less like a harmless quirk and more like the edge piece of a puzzle I'm not ready to fit into place.

Chapter Five

I dress for dinner in blousy linen pants and a sky-blue silk tank. Dad expects people to look nice when he cooks—at least he used to. After the ham-sandwich fiasco, I'm not sure what to expect.

When Scout pads after me, I don't have the heart to leave her in the cottage alone. The dog has been clingy since I returned from town, eyes fixed on the door as though Addie might walk through any second.

Up at the house, I find Dad in the kitchen, sleeves rolled, moving with the easy rhythm of a man who knows his way around a meal. The French doors are open to the evening breeze, soft jazz drifts from the speaker, and a bottle of red breathes on the counter. For a moment, the years rewind—I'm home for one of his legendary dinner parties, when senators, high-ranking judges, even the governor himself gathered at Hollis Sutherlin's table. Back when he ruled this kitchen like a king.

He glances up and smiles at me, the familiar twinkle lighting his hazel eyes—so like my own.

"You look lovely." He leans in to kiss my cheek, the familiar spicy, sweet scent of his Bay Rum aftershave clinging to his skin.

I take in his khaki slacks and cheerful plaid shirt, one button askew. "Thanks. You're looking sharp yourself." I reach for a glass and pour myself some wine. "How can I help?"

Dad nods at the bag of fresh greens from Publix. "Start on the salad, if you want."

"Got it." I pull cucumbers and tomatoes from the fridge, the cold produce firm beneath my fingers.

Dad turns back to the mixing bowl where he's working on the secret blend of cheeses and spices for his famous grits casserole. "How's the investigation going? Any leads on finding Addie?"

"Not yet. Not that I've heard. Even though I'm not officially on the case, I hope Boone will have the decency to keep me in the loop."

"He will." Dad runs a stick of butter around the casserole dish. "I don't know why you're so hard on Franklin. He's one of the good guys."

I press my lips thin, biting back my response. Dad doesn't know the half of it.

"I hope you're giving Clay a good hard look. Does he have an alibi?"

The suspicion in his tone stops me cold. My knife stills against the cutting board, every nerve on alert. "Why do you ask? Do you think he might've hurt her?"

"You know the rule—always look to the husband first."

My eyes narrow. "What aren't you saying, Dad?"

He pours the creamy grits mixture into the dish, steam curling upward. "Just that Clay's a charmer. All the women in town worship him. Most of the men too. Clay and Addie are the town's sweetheart couple . . ." His voice trails off.

"But . . ." I gesture with the knife. "Go on."

"I don't want to overstep. Addie's *your* best friend. What do you think of him?"

The words stick in my throat. I shouldn't say this. But it's the truth. "I've never told anyone this, not even Addie. But something about him has always felt off. People who shine that bright usually have shadows. And Clay Dalton strikes me as the type who polishes his halo before bed."

I drop my gaze, letting the steady chop of cucumbers fill the silence. "He claims he was at home, cleaning his guns for hunting season. A convenient story, except that he was alone. I doubt anyone can verify his whereabouts."

Dad slips the casserole into the oven and straightens, scanning the kitchen as though searching for a misplaced thought. "Whose whereabouts?"

A chill ripples through me. "Clay's. We were talking about Addie's disappearance."

He blinks, then pastes on a smile that doesn't quite reach his eyes. "Of course. That's what I meant." He turns back to the counter, dusting the salmon with paprika and dill as if the lapse never happened.

I stare at him, my throat tight. How much longer can I pretend these slips are harmless?

Dad lifts the plate of fish. "These are ready for the grill."

I gather our wineglasses and follow him outside to the bluestone patio.

Once the grill is preheated, Dad lays the salmon steaks on the grate and lowers the lid with a metallic thunk. He turns his back to me, his gaze drifting over the river, the water catching the last streaks of sunset. "I heard they might tear down the old boathouse in the park."

"You mean the Tide House? Why?"

"Because it's dangerous—rotten wood, rusted-out roof, boardwalk half submerged." His eyes go distant, voice softening with nostalgia. "Shame, really. Back in the day, it was the heart of Tidewell. Fourth of July picnics, fall festivals . . . The whole town would be there. I learned to fish off that dock before I was big enough to bait my own hook." He rubs at the corner of his eye as if brushing away a speck of dust. "You kids used to play tag on that porch till your mama called you in for supper."

"Capture the flag," I correct him with a faint smile. "We did all the rites of passage in that boathouse—first kisses, first tastes of alcohol."

"Don't remind me," Dad mutters, though a ghost of a grin tugs at his mouth as he reaches for his wine. "It's a part of Tidewell history—built in 1898 by the local watermen's association. Back then, oystermen and crabbers would unload their day's catch right there on the dock, selling it straight to the townsfolk. Sometimes, you could smell the brine and hear the shuckers' knives clicking before you even rounded the bend. The boathouse was one of the few structures left standing after Hurricane Celeste roared through here in 1976. Folks called it a miracle, though the old-timers swore it was the craftsmanship—thick pilings driven deep into the creek bed and good timber that could bend without breaking."

I follow his gaze into the darkening water. The old boathouse sits in the distance, its weathered siding leaning just enough to hint at surrender, the tide creeping higher against its posts as if testing its resolve. "Seems a crime to tear it down. Why not fix it up instead?"

"The county says it'd cost too much to save."

"Why do they call it the Tide House? I can't believe I never knew, never thought to ask."

He shrugs. "Who knows? One person says it, the rest repeat it. That's how small towns work. Before long, it's the only name anyone remembers."

Dad lifts the salmon from the grill, the smoky aroma trailing after him as we head inside. I top off our wine while he plates the fish, salad, and generous scoops of steaming grits casserole.

We settle in the breakfast alcove at one end of the old farm table, its surface worn smooth by decades of family meals. A fat pillar candle casts a warm, flickering glow between us, softening the lines of my father's face and pooling light over the simple spread. Beyond the open French doors, the night air drifts in with the faint briny scent of the river.

"Have you seen your mom lately?" Dad asks, forking off a bite of salmon.

I drag my fork through my grits. "Um . . . no. I haven't talked to her in forever. You know that."

He grunts. "Well, it's high time you two made up."

Dad has never gotten over the breakup of his marriage. He's old-school—where he comes from, tragedy is supposed to weld families together, not rip them apart.

"We're not little girls who had a squabble, Dad. I'll never forgive Mom for what she did. She walked out on us when we needed her the most. Now that she has found herself a new family, she doesn't need us anymore."

Dad and I have always been close. No one was surprised when I insisted on living with him after the divorce. He was the steady one—the one who made sure I got to school on time, kept the fridge stocked, remembered the little things Mom never bothered with. He might have been strict, but he showed up. And in my book, showing up is everything.

"You're still her daughter, Bug."

"Tell that to Roxie. She has two new daughters now," I say, shoveling grits into my mouth.

For a while we eat in silence—the good kind. A cool fall breeze drifts through the open doors, jazz humming low, the table laid with simple but beautiful food. For just a moment, it feels almost normal.

Summoning the courage, I swallow my last bite of salmon and set down my napkin. "There's something you should know. Grayson and I—"

The slam of the back door makes me jump. I groan inwardly as Judd strides in from the mudroom, his voice already sharp. "So it's true. The prodigal daughter's finally come home. Took your best friend disappearing to get you here."

I glare at my older brother, my pulse ticking faster. "Nice to see you too."

Scout trots over to greet him, tail wagging, oblivious to the tension. Judd crouches to scratch her head. "Cool dog. Did you rescue her . . . him?" He sneaks a peek at the dog's behind. "Her."

"She belongs to Addie. I'm keeping her for Clay."

"Oh. I see." Judd's gaze flicks around the room, casual on the surface but sharp underneath. "Where's your sidekick? You leave Grayson at home?"

The jab lands like a pebble in my shoe—small but irritating. I shove my plate aside and lean forward on my elbows. "I was about to break the news to Dad. Grayson and I are divorced."

Judd's eyebrows shoot up. "Really? Did you finally get sick of his classical music?"

"Actually, he had an affair with a concert violinist. Or at least that's the story I tell. It sounds more glamorous than the truth. She's just another attorney at his law firm. Same difference. Both think they're God's gift and carry a case everywhere."

Judd never liked my husband. The night before our wedding —in a rare moment of brotherly concern—he'd tried to talk me out of marrying him.

"I'm sorry, Lane. That sucks," Judd says, yanking open the fridge and grabbing a beer. "Even though I couldn't stand the prick."

"I admit, you were right about him." I risk a glance at Dad. His expression is a mix of hurt and surprise, like I've just spoiled the ending of a new release from his favorite mystery author.

"Grayson cheated on you?" he asks, incredulous.

I nod. "I'm sorry, Dad. I know how much you enjoyed his company."

He reaches for my hand, his grip warm but faintly trembling. "I'm sorry for you, Laney Bug. I wish you had told me sooner." Confusion knits his brow. "You didn't tell me sooner, did you?"

A laugh escapes me. Could he really have forgotten something so important? "No, Dad. I wanted to tell you in person."

Dad shrinks back in his chair, suddenly looking small—like a lost little boy.

I lean in, lowering my voice. "What's wrong, Dad? Are you okay?"

He musters a soft smile. "Yes, sweetheart. Just . . . suddenly very tired."

"Then go to bed. I'll clean up the kitchen."

He glances at the mess, hesitant. "Are you sure?"

"Positive. Since you cooked, it's only fair I clean up."

He pushes back from the table, his frame more slouched than I remember. I watch him shuffle down the hallway, disappearing into the shadows.

I gather our empty plates and carry them to the kitchen. "Why didn't you tell me?" I say to my brother through clenched teeth.

"Tell you what? That Dad's not twenty-five anymore," he says, popping a cap off another beer.

I drop the plates on the counter with a clatter. "About Dad's memory slipping."

Judd exhales hard. "Slipping? Try swan-diving off a cliff, no helmet, no parachute."

I turn on the water, running my fingers under the stream until the temperature is right. "Has he seen a doctor?"

He snorts. "You know Dad. He refuses to go."

"So you're just ignoring it?" I say, rinsing plates and sliding them into the dishwasher.

"I've spoken to Dr. Jenkins. He'll need a full neurological workup to confirm Alzheimer's."

My head snaps up. "So? What're we waiting for?"

"No one wants to deal with it, Lane. Not Dad. Not me. Nobody. Easier to just . . . let it run its course."

I fill the sink with hot, soapy water for the pots and pans, scrubbing harder than I need to. "Aren't there meds that can slow the progression?"

"How would I know? Do I look like a doctor?" He drops his empty beer bottle in the recycling bin with a clink. "Don't come back here stirring up trouble. Dad's not one of your cases. He doesn't need investigating."

"Then what does he need?"

He shrugs, the motion careless, but his voice a little too firm. "A memory care unit—eventually. But that's not now. He's still fine. He hasn't gotten lost driving. Pays his bills. Knows my name."

I point to the fridge. "There was no food here when I arrived. Someone has to look out for him."

"And who's that someone? I stop by when I can, but I'm busy with my own life."

"Yeah? That many boat motors needing your magic touch? Or are you just hiding out in a shed until the world forgets you exist?" I give Judd grief about his profession, like being a detective makes me any better. Truth is, he's one of the most sought-after yacht mechanics in Virginia—maybe the whole East Coast.

"I gotta go," he says, heading for the mudroom. "Do us all a favor—go back to solving crimes in Richmond. You're neither needed nor wanted here."

My throat burns. Why does he always know how to push all my buttons at once? I was doing just fine in Richmond—no forgetful father, no Bramble twins, no brother getting under my skin. But now, with Dad's memory slipping and Judd brushing it off, a nagging thought takes root, stubborn as crabgrass. I might not be able to leave when I find Addie.

Chapter Six

Dark thoughts of Addie won't let me sleep. Around three, after hours of tossing and turning, I give up and make coffee. I have a job to do. Sleep can wait. I step onto the porch, where the salt-tinged air presses cool and damp against my skin.

I can no longer ignore my instincts. We're past twenty-four hours now, and nothing has surfaced. The realization slams into my chest like a fist—Addie might be dead. Who would hurt her? My Addie, the kindest person I know.

Screw that. This is no longer a quick trip home. I'm not leaving Tidewell until I find Addie—alive or dead. Even if it takes weeks.

If Addie's body turns up, I'll hunt the bastard down and make him pay. While my gut keeps pinging on Clay, I can't charge in guns blazing. He's Tidewell's crown prince—untouchable to most —and an accusation with no proof would burn bridges and set half the town against me.

When the first rays of dawn cast a pink hue over the marsh, I pull on athletic clothes and take Scout out for a run in Founders Park.

As I'm passing the main house, I notice the light glowing from Dad's upstairs bedroom window. He's another reason for me to stay in Tidewell. I'm not like Judd. I can't ignore the memory lapses. Dad needs help, and I'm going to make sure he gets it. The idea of a disease eating away at my father's brilliant mind unsettles me almost as much as Addie's disappearance.

After a long run, I shower, feed the dog, and drive to town. I'm waiting outside the salon—two pumpkin-spiced lattes in hand—when my old friend Trina arrives to open the salon at eight. As co-owners of Crown & Glory, she and Addie spend more time together than they do with their husbands. If anyone can shed light on Addie's state of mind in those last days, it's Trina.

I haven't seen her in years, but the warmth in Trina's brown eyes tugs me straight back to late-night heart-to-hearts and whispered confessions. She was always the keeper of our secrets—no matter how juicy. That loyalty, paired with her killer sense of style, has earned her the title of most sought-after stylist in town.

Trina pulls me into a hug that smells faintly of hairspray and vanilla. "Thank God you're here. You need to help these clowns find Addie." Noticing Scout at my side, she drops to her knees, hugging the dog's neck. "I'm so happy to see you, girl. How're you holding up without your mama? Wait a minute." She looks up at me, her expression grief-stricken. "Why is Scout with you? Did they find Addie?"

"Not yet. It's a long story." I hand her a pumpkin-spiced latte. "Do you have time to talk?"

"Yes! Of course. But I need to stay busy, or I'll worry myself sick." With her free hand, Trina slips the elastic from my ponytail and lets out a low whistle. "When's the last time you had this mop cut?"

I laugh. "I don't remember. Years."

"I can tell." She spins the stylist's chair towards me. "Plant it."

Running my hand over my hair, I picture the Trina of our teenage years—smearing drugstore gloss on our lips, choosing our outfits for Friday night football games. "Thanks. But I don't have time for a haircut today."

"Too bad. I can't, in good conscience, let you walk around looking like that," she says, snapping a cape around me.

I lower into the chair with a sigh. "If you insist. But just take off a little."

"Mm-hmm." Trina's noncommittal hum says she'll do exactly what she wants to my hair.

"What're you doing about Addie's clients?" I ask.

Trina hikes up the chair and gives my hair a quick mist from a spray bottle. "Fitting them in whenever possible. I have a sick feeling about this, Laney. Addie wouldn't take off without telling me. And she sure as hell wouldn't leave her clients hanging." She points her comb at Scout, lounging at my feet. "And that dog? She never goes anywhere without her."

Tears prick the backs of my eyes. It's one thing for me to think it. Another thing entirely to hear someone else say it. "I agree, it doesn't look good. Is there anything you can tell me that might help me find her?"

Trina drags the comb through my wet hair, the teeth catching on a tangle. "I already told Sheriff Boone everything I know. Which is basically nothing."

"Was she having problems at home?" I ask lightly, testing the water, unsure how she feels about Clay.

"She seemed fine." Trina avoids my gaze in the mirror, but I catch the flicker across her face—there and gone before I can pin it down.

"Look, Trina." I lower my voice, even though we're alone in the salon. "You're the most trustworthy person I've ever met, but this is one time it's okay to break that trust. If you know something, you have to tell me. It might save her life."

For a heartbeat, Trina goes still, comb suspended midair. I lean forward, certain she's about to speak. But then Trina inhales a deep breath, the kind meant to steady herself, and resumes cutting.

"I don't know anything, Lane," she says finally, her voice small but firm. "The answers lie with that dog. How did Scout end up with you?"

I warn myself to be patient. Trina's fierce loyalty to Addie isn't something I'll break easily. "Addie called me the night she went missing. My phone was off, so I didn't get the message until the next morning. A buddy at Richmond PD pulled the tower hit. The signal registered at a tower near Patriots Landing Marina. I went out there to poke around and found Scout by the road near the Bayview dump."

Trina tenses, her eyes fixed on the scissors. "She usually walks Scout around the town square at night. What was she doing all the way out there?"

"That's the million-dollar question," I mutter. Trina knows something—I can feel it—but she's hiding behind her poker face. But I can wait. I'll pry the answers out soon enough.

Trina shifts into autopilot, layering and thinning my hair while chatting nonstop about her two little girls—birthdays, school projects, ballet recitals. As much as I want to hear about her life, my mind is locked on Addie.

She spritzes my hair with styling product before blowing it dry. When she finishes, I barely recognize the woman staring back from the mirror. My hair now has shape—soft layers that frame my face, catching the light so it seems warmer.

Trina steps back, cocking her head. "Your hair's still something else, Lane. Rich mahogany brown with those natural golden streaks—women would kill for it." She leans in, her chin lightly resting on my shoulder, our eyes meeting in the mirror. "I always thought you were the prettiest girl in our class."

I arch a brow. "Seriously? Not Addie?"

"Addie was gorgeous in a flashy sort of way—the cheerleader type, perky blonde with that perfect little nose. But you . . ." Trina tilts her head. "You're elegant—high cheekbones, intense hazel eyes."

Sadness tugs at my faint smile. Trina doesn't even realize she's just spoken about Addie in the past tense.

When I reach for my wallet, Trina waves me off. "On the house. You can repay me by finding Addie."

"Don't worry. I'll find her." I press my cheek to hers. "Call me if you think of anything else. Or if you just want to talk." I hold her gaze for a beat longer than necessary, letting her know I see what she's not saying.

Addie's mother lives on Dogwood Drive, a few streets south of the town square. Behind her white clapboard house sits a converted carriage building that serves as headquarters for her bustling catering business.

Everyone calls her Mama Jean, but she was more than just a mother hen to me. She was my stand-in mom after the divorce—the one I could always count on for a ride, a listening ear, and a plate of cookies. She knew about the boys, the awkward girl problems, even my college worries.

Mama Jean was the only one who believed in my artistic streak, certain my pen-and-ink doodles could become a career. She pushed me toward art school at VCU. But one semester in, I learned the truth—I have no talent. Turns out I'm better with lines that don't smudge, the kind you find in a case file.

When I pull into the driveway, I spot Mama Jean on the porch, rocking like she's trying to outpace her own worry, eyes on the street as if waiting for word of her daughter to appear.

Scout's ears prick, recognition sparking. As soon as I open my door, the dog leaps over my lap and bolts up the sidewalk. She plants her paws squarely in Mama Jean's lap, smothering her with eager licks.

Mama Jean hugs the dog, then eases her aside and pushes herself out of the chair. "Do you have news?"

"No, ma'am. Not yet." I take her hands in mine. "How're you holding up?"

"I'm a wreck, honestly. Can't eat. Can't sleep. I can't even cook —and I'm a caterer for goodness' sake. I keep imagining the worst. And the visions of all the terrible things that might've happened to my sweet baby . . ." She shakes her head. "They're tormenting me."

I don't tell her those same visions kept me up all night. "We're gonna find her, Mama Jean. I promise."

Easing her hands free of mine, she takes a shaky breath and reaches for the doorknob. "Let me get this dog some water. Would you like something? I just made a pitcher of lemonade."

I lick my lips. "That sounds delicious. I could never resist your lemonade."

Scout trails her inside, tail wagging, certain that a treat awaits in Mama Jean's kitchen. She adores Addie, and losing her only child would destroy her. I sink into a rocker, close my eyes, and whisper a prayer for Addie's safe return.

Mama Jean returns with two tall glasses of lemonade, pale yellow with a sprig of mint floating on top. I take a sip, moaning softly. "You never miss. Just the right balance of sweet and tart."

"How did Scout end up with you?" Mama Jean asks.

I repeat the story about Addie's message, her phone's last ping near the marina, and finding Scout out by the dump.

Her brows knit, mouth pinched as she listens. "The police didn't tell me all that. Wonder what else they're keeping from me. Why didn't you take the dog home to Clay?"

"He asked me to keep her, said he couldn't deal with a high-energy dog right now. I don't mind, honestly. She's good company." I smile at the dog, now curled at Mama Jean's feet.

"If you get tired of her, bring her to me. That dog's part of this family too."

"I will. But she's fine for now." I take another sip and set down the glass. "How has Addie seemed lately? Anything unusual?"

Mama Jean settles back in her chair. "I didn't see much of her this summer. The few times we managed dinner, she seemed . . . distracted." She hesitates, eyes dropping to her lap. "I could tell something was weighing on her, but you know how Addie guards her heart."

I smile to myself. Addie always put up a good front no matter what storm was brewing in her world. "Do you think she's happy with Clay?"

Mama Jean's head snaps up. "What makes you ask that?"

"I think Clay's a jackass. Obviously, I'd never admit that to Addie. Maybe it's just me. Maybe I resent him for taking my spot as the most important person in Addie's life." I grin, but it feels a little forced.

She chuckles. "Just so you know—that spot belongs to me." Her blue eyes darken, something unspoken flickering there. "But I know what you mean about Clay. Women flock to him, and he soaks it up. He may wear the badge of a married man, but that doesn't mean he's above temptation. I've lived long enough to know better."

I shift in my chair, uneasy with her bluntness. "That's not exactly the kind of man you want your daughter to build a life with."

Mama Jean gives her head a slow shake. "No, it's not. Truth is, I'm not sure I'd recognize the signs if she was having problems. She's always smiling, always putting on that happy face no matter how rough things get." She leans closer, her voice dropping to a whisper. "I always thought Ben was the one for her. Life would've been simpler that way."

I cut my eyes at her. "Whatever happened between those two? Addie never would tell me."

"She broke up with him before she left for cosmetology school in Atlanta. She wanted to be free to experience life before settling down. She saw what the hard life of a waterman did to her father. And she wanted more for herself than being a waterman's wife. Turns out, wanting more and getting more aren't always the same thing. And sometimes, wanting more is exactly what gets you hurt."

Chapter Seven

What our small town lacks in sophistication, it makes up for in colorful history.

In the early seventies, a local sailor named Amos Greeley returned home from Vietnam with a rusty old navy tugboat he'd somehow acquired on the Mekong Delta. To this day, folks still argue over how he got it. Some say he won it in a poker game, others claim he inherited it from a fallen comrade, and a few insist he took it from the navy fleet without permission. Whatever the truth, Amos pulled into Tidewell's city marina looking for a place to tie up.

There wasn't a slip big enough for the hulking beast, so they stuck him at the end of the dock—past the last numbered berth. Out there, with nothing but water on three sides, Amos rigged a canvas tent over the tug's wide-open stern, hammered together a bar top from salvaged wood, and started pouring drinks for anyone willing to climb aboard.

He called it Slip 99. Some say the number honored the ninety-nine souls lost from his division. Others swear it came from a rusted ammo crate he'd turned into a barstool. Either way, Slip 99 became a gathering spot for fishermen, boat mechanics, and brokenhearted locals who found comfort in Amos's rough wisdom and strong pours.

Then came the summer of '76. Hurricane Celeste tore up the coast and laid waste to Tidewell. The marina was shredded—boats sunk, boardwalks mangled, everything gone except Amos's tug. Battered but afloat, it clung to the last remaining sliver of dock, the old bar sign swaying defiantly in the wind. Amos himself wasn't so lucky. At least, that's the story. No body was ever found.

When the town rebuilt the marina, they honored Amos the only way they knew how—by replacing the tug with a two-story wooden bar at the edge of the dock, still named Slip 99.

Regulars say the drinks taste saltier now, the stories run deeper. And on stormy nights, some swear they hear Amos's gravelly voice hollering for last call over the wind.

These days, Cooter McNair mans the bar—a crusty fixture who once washed dishes for Amos and now calls himself "Old Salt of Slip 99."

The dive is popular with the locals for special occasions—birthday dinners, first dates, even the occasional marriage proposal. Dad and I used to come here for Saturday breakfasts, Sunday brunches after church, and more lunches than I can count. Back in high school, my girlfriends and I claimed the corner table by the window whenever there was something to celebrate—report cards, team victories, college acceptances.

Today, the place is packed, as expected on a Saturday in September—mounted televisions behind the bar and in the corners of the dining area broadcasting SEC football. Fortunately, I only have to wait a few minutes before two spots open up at the bar. I slip onto one, and Scout hops onto the other.

With a quick glance over his shoulder, Cooter yells at me. "Hey, Lady! No dogs allowed." He does a double take, zeroing in on the pink collar with her name stitched in white. "Scout?" His gaze lifts to me, narrowing as he takes me in. "Laney? Is that you?" He turns toward me, grinning. "Well, I'll be a monkey's uncle. It's been so long since I've seen you, I didn't even recognize you."

"Good to see you, Cooter. You haven't changed a bit."

"Ha. Haven't you heard? Nothing ever changes around here." His smile fades. "You're in on the search for Addie." Not a question—he already knows. Slip 99 is ground zero for Tidewell gossip.

"I am."

"Any updates?" He slings a rag over his shoulder, the simple motion at odds with the worry in his eyes.

"Not yet. I'm keeping Scout for Clay until we find her."

A customer at the far end of the bar waves him down. Cooter lifts a finger, signaling he'll be right there, then slides a menu across the bar to me. "Know what you want, or need a minute to decide?"

I nudge the menu back toward him. "House salad, half dozen raw oysters, and a burger patty for my friend here." I tug gently on Scout's ear. "She's not much on lettuce, but I bet she could slurp oysters like a pro."

Cooter chuckles. "I bet she could. I'll get your order in. Shouldn't be too long," he says, hurrying off to assist the other customer.

Another bartender—a pretty blonde with sparkling blue eyes and the kind of curves that guarantee good tips—sets a small bowl of water on the bar in front of Scout. "Hey there. I'm Frances Bell, but most folks call me Frankie." She flashes a grin. "But only if you don't snap your fingers at me."

I return the smile. "Lane Sutherlin. Nice to meet you, Frankie. And I would never dare snap at you."

She hooks four fingers through a row of mugs and starts the taps flowing. "I know who you are. Scout and Addie come in all the time. Addie's always bragging about you."

I place my hand over my heart. "She is?"

"Yep. She really misses you." She delivers the beers to a group of customers down the bar, then circles back, her tone softer now. "I'm worried sick about her. I sure hope you find her soon."

"We will," I say with more confidence than I feel.

Frankie nods toward the swinging door that leads to the kitchen. "Your order will be out in a minute. Can I get you something to drink while you wait?"

"I'll have a limeade, please," I say—their specialty nonalcoholic fix.

The food arrives a few minutes later—my salad and oysters on two plates and Scout's hamburger cut into neat bites on a platter. She doesn't wait for an invitation, muzzle already down.

I fork into the salad, ears tuned to the conversations buzzing around me. Behind me, a table of men are glued to the Alabama–Georgia game, voices rising with every play. They sound so familiar, I risk a glance over my shoulder. Three of the four are old classmates. Eli Morgan—sweet but forever awkward. Colt Drummond—the class bad boy who never outgrew the title. And Beau Ramsey—once a tennis prodigy, too undisciplined to go pro.

Even after all these years, I'd know their voices anywhere. Colt's busy laying bets on the afternoon games, Eli keeps whining he doesn't have the cash, and Beau jokes his wife would kill him if she caught him gambling.

Bored with their play-by-play, I shift my attention to the couple beside me—only to catch a snippet of whispered sex talk that makes my cheeks burn. I block them out fast.

Scout polishes off the burger, hops down from the stool, and curls between my feet, snoring softly against the bar's wood rail. I'm slurping the last oyster when Colt's voice cuts through the din.

"Ben! About time. We were waiting for you to order."

"Why the long face, bro?" Beau chimes in.

"He's upset about Addie," Colt says, too loud, like he's breaking news.

"Ah, man." Beau snorts. "Don't tell me you're still hung up on her. She's married. Time to move on."

Ben drops into an empty chair with a heavy thud. "I'm not still hung up on her. We're friends. I'm just . . . worried. Aren't y'all?"

Eli speaks for the first time, his voice quiet but strong. "Yeah. She's always been nice to me. I'd have flunked out of high school if not for Addie. She tutored me in nearly every subject. Never asked for a dime."

"That's true," Colt says, unusually thoughtful. "She used to cover for me when I cut class. Lied to Mr. Dillard like it was nothing."

Beau is next. "She brought us a gourmet dinner when the baby was born—salmon, risotto, those little lemon bars my wife still raves about."

Ben lets out a heavy sigh. "That's Addie, always helping other people. Never thinking about herself."

Their conversation hits me harder than I expect. Grown men—laughing, swearing, arguing over football—but when Addie's name surfaces, they soften, boys again, remembering the girl who once made them feel seen.

I push back my stool and cross the room to them with Scout on my heels.

Ben looks up first. "Lane?"

"Hey, guys." I lift a hand, hoping they don't notice the wobble in my voice.

Scout practically leaps into Ben's lap, and he catches her like it's second nature. "Hey, girl," he murmurs, scratching behind her ears.

I arch a brow. "You two seem awfully friendly. Do you see a lot of Addie and Scout?"

"Of course," Ben says, still stroking her fur. "I see them out walking all the time."

The familiar way he handles her feels like more than neighborly affection. But I let it slide. "Is there anything any of you can tell me about Addie that might help me find her?"

Colt's eyes widen. "That's right. I heard you were a big-city detective now. Are you working the case?"

"Not officially. But I'm investigating. And I *will* find her."

"I hope you do," Eli says. "I don't know why anyone would hurt her."

"Me either," Beau says. "Must've been a random act. Some stranger, maybe."

While the others speculate, I keep one eye on Ben. He doesn't chime in. He sits stone-faced, jaw tight, heat radiating off him. Anger? Or something worse? Guilt?

I think about what Mama Jean said earlier. *I always thought Ben was the one for her. Life might've been easier that way.* Easier . . . or messier? Was something still going on between them?

Either way—now's not the time to interrogate Ben. And I won't find Addie by sitting around making small talk, no matter how good the oysters are here.

I scribble my number on a napkin and slide it across the table. "Call me if anything comes to mind. Even if it feels small."

Ben doesn't meet my eyes, but his hand lingers on Scout a beat too long. She watches him as we leave, ears cocked, head tilted. She trusts him. Addie did too, once. And so did I. We were close in high school—back when he and Addie dated. But can I still trust him? I'm not sure.

Chapter Eight

I spend much of the afternoon reacquainting myself with my hometown. Parking on the square, I head straight for Sweet Tilly's and their heavenly gourmet donuts. The flavors change with the season, and today they have my favorite—glazed lemon blueberry. I order two—one for me, one for Scout. Giving that much sugar to a dog is probably a terrible idea, but after what she's been through, she deserves it.

The girl behind the counter can't be more than sixteen, working part-time after school and on weekends. When I show her a photo of Addie, she immediately recognizes her from the paper.

"Yeah, I heard. Scary, the way she just vanished. She's been in a few times. I haven't been working here long enough to know if she's a regular."

"Thanks anyway." I leave my number just in case.

I polish off my donut—it's every bit as good as I remember—and buy a half dozen more to take back to the farm. Dad will fuss about the sugar, but he could stand a little fattening up.

My next stop is Tidewell's only women's boutique—Birdie & Belle. The place has had a serious glow-up since I was last in. Fresh paint, cozy chairs, curated displays. Even the racks have leveled up—sleek dresses and tailored jackets instead of the frumpy polyester that used to scream *ladies' luncheon.*

The young woman behind the counter looks familiar, though it takes me a moment to place her. "Hallie! I almost didn't recognize you. You're so . . . gorgeous."

Gone is the simple, sweet girl I remember. She's dressed head to toe in the latest trends, hair glossy, confidence radiating. Hallie was dating Tommy at the time of his accident. She was a senior when I was just a freshman, but grief bonded us in a way age didn't.

She comes from behind the counter. "Laney, so good to see you. I'm the new owner. What do you think of the changes?"

"I approve," I say with a glance of appreciation around the shop. "How'd you manage to bring Birdie & Belle into the twenty-first century?"

She laughs. "Trust me, it wasn't easy." She studies me with kind eyes. "I think of you often."

"I heard you were helping look for Addie. I'm worried sick. She's the only stylist who's ever been able to tame these curls." She tugs at the wavy blonde ponytail on her shoulder. "Any leads?"

I give my head a grim shake. "Not yet." Scribbling my number on the back of one of her business cards, I place it on the counter. "In case you think of anything that might help."

"For sure!" Hallie walks me to the door. "Come back when you're not pressed for time. We'll grab a coffee and catch up."

I hesitate before stepping out. Seeing her stirs memories—not just the bad ones but flashes of that last golden summer before the accident.

"I'd like that," I say softly.

Next door, the barista at the Salty Bean Café is passing out sample cups of their fall lineup—spiced apple chai, maple sea salt latte, and the inevitable pumpkin spice cold foam Brew. I down all three, the smell of cinnamon and nutmeg trailing after me as I head down the block.

At Turner's Hardware & Marine, the entire staff knows Addie, but no one can offer a single lead. Just the same hollow sympathy I've been hearing all day.

My last stop is Whaley's Pharmacy—the town's old standby, still delivering prescriptions and serving the best ice cream floats at the soda fountain in the back.

I decide to splurge. Why not? I've already blown my diet for the day. If I keep this up, I'll put on more than the few extra pounds Morales and Boone say I need.

Marge, the counter attendant, spots Scout right away and pours a little extra float in a bowl just for her. She's clearly a fan of Addie—says she orders lunch from here all the time—but she has no useful information to offer.

"She was always cheerful and smiling," Marge says with a sad shake of her head. "If she had any problems, she never showed it."

I nod, thank her, and head back to the car. Tidewell wears its secrets well. But someone's hiding something, and I intend to find out who.

When I arrive back at River Birch, I stop by the main house to drop off the donuts. Dad's car sits in the driveway, but the place is empty. I leave the box on the kitchen counter and walk down to the water. His ancient tub is still tied to the dock—engine cold. Who knows if the damn thing even starts?

The cottage is unlocked. I'm almost certain I locked it when I left this morning, but nothing appears disturbed, and there's no sign of Dad.

My stomach knots.

Returning to the house, I search from top to bottom—under beds, behind doors, even in closets. When I call his number, I hear the muffled sound of ringing. I tap and listen, following the tone to the linen closet. The phone's buried in a stack of towels, battery alive. Now I'm not just uneasy. I'm really worried.

I call Judd. He answers on the third ring, sounding annoyed. "What's up, Lane? I'm in the middle of something."

"So am I—a missing person case. Make that two. I can't find Dad. His car and boat are here. I found his phone in the linen closet. Do you know his passcode?"

"Five-five-five-five—not very original. I wouldn't worry too much. He hides things, afraid someone might steal them."

I thumb in the code and scroll through Dad's messages. "Nothing new in the past twenty-four hours. Has he done this before?"

"A couple of times. He just wanders off, but he always comes home. Keep looking—he couldn't have gone far."

"Aren't you gonna come help me?"

"Nope. I'm busy. Your turn to deal with it."

"Thanks for nothing," I snap. "I just hope he didn't get hit by a car."

I pocket Dad's phone and flee the house, heart pounding. Scout races at my side, matching my panic stride for stride, as if she can feel it too.

After combing every inch of the property, I get in the car and inch my way along Riverside Drive back toward town—ignoring the angry horn blasts from drivers behind me. I pass through the brick gates at Founders Park and follow the winding road toward the water. I remember Dad mentioning wanting to go fishing at the old boathouse—the Tide House. As I round the last curve, I spot a stooped figure on the dock—faded bucket hat, fishing rod in hand, leaning against a piling.

Dad! Thank God!

At first glance, he appears asleep. I shield my eyes from the sun and squint for a better look. He's perched at the edge of the dock, eyes wide open, fixed on the water like he's caught in a trance.

I get out of the car and walk slowly toward him, not wanting to startle him.

"Dad?" I call out in a soft voice. "Are you okay?"

He turns—surprised. "Oh! Hey, sweetheart. What're you doing here?"

"I've been looking for you. You didn't leave a note or tell anyone where you were going."

"I'm just fishing. Look what I caught." He opens the cooler beside him, revealing a few undersized redfish that are surely below the legal-size limit.

I open my mouth to scold him, but the sound of frantic scratching stops me—Scout at the boathouse door, pawing and whimpering.

I rush to her. "What is it, girl?" I try the knob, but it won't budge.

Dad shuffles over, concern clouding his expression. "What's wrong, Laney Bug?"

"I'm not sure. Hold the dog for me while I break it open."

He barely has time to step back before I slam my heel into the door. The old wood gives way on the second try, splintering around the lock and swinging wide open.

The smell hits me first. Then I see her. Golden hair, tangled and dull, spread across the rotting boardwalk. Her skin is pale, lips parted. Around her neck, faint but unmistakable, is a narrow dark band. Something pulled tight. The spark that was Addie— gone.

Scout howls, trembling, clawing at the ground.

"Don't go in there!" I shout at Dad, yanking Scout back by the collar and dragging her over to the Bronco. She claws at the door when I close her inside, her cries like a siren through the glass.

My heart splinters as I turn my back on her.

I've seen my share of dead bodies, but never someone I loved. My stomach lurches. I make it to the edge of the boardwalk before I drop to my knees and vomit over the side.

I sit back on my haunches, chest heaving, bile stinging the back of my throat—the taste of grief I can't swallow down. The world blurs—sunlight on the water, the creak of the dock, the muffled cries of Scout from inside the car. I wipe my mouth with the back of my hand and try to steady my breathing. I can't go back in there. Not yet.

I glance behind me at Dad, who hasn't moved. He stands frozen near the boathouse door, an arm looped around a piling—the only thing holding him up.

I tug Dad's phone out of my pocket and open the call log. Boone is at the top of his favorites list. His best friend. The sheriff. The man Dad trusts most—maybe more than he trusts me. Boone will take a call from Dad long before he takes one from me.

He picks up on the second ring. "Afternoon, Judge."

I open my mouth, but no words come.

"Hello?" Boone's tone sharpens. "Hollis?"

"It's Lane," I manage, my throat raw. "I found Addie at the Tide House."

There's a pause, long enough to feel it. I glance over at the car. Scout's nose is pressed to the window.

"Someone killed her, Sheriff," I say quietly. "There are ligature marks around her neck. Hard to say if this was the murder scene . . . or if someone dumped her here."

I lower the phone and press it to my chest, like I can hold myself together by sheer force. But the truth hits me hard and final. Nothing about this will ever be okay.

Chapter Nine

Dad and I stand like sentries at the boathouse door, unmoving, staring ahead but not really seeing.

In my mind's eye, two little girls in matching yellow polka dot bathing suits squeal with delight as they chase each other down this very dock. We cannonball off the end, again and again, laughing at everything and nothing.

Addie. My sister in every way but blood. Keeper of my secrets. Finisher of my sentences. My safe place.

And now she's gone.

It doesn't feel real.

It can't be real.

Please, someone, wake me from this nightmare.

Sirens wail, shattering the illusion.

Dad's eyes are fixed on the body now. "Who is that?" he asks, voice flat. His gaze doesn't move from Addie, and I wonder if he, too, is caught in a memory—reliving another body, another tragedy, another senseless loss.

"That's Addie, Dad," I say gently. "My best friend. Remember? She was missing?"

He shakes his head as if to clear it, then looks up at me. "Yes. Yes, of course." His tone is heavy, worn down with grief.

A long line of patrol cars rounds the bend, gravel spitting from their tires, a haze of dust rising behind them. They skid to uneven stops around us, doors flying open as deputies spill out—Clay striding in front, Boone bringing up the rear.

I step in front of the doorway, blocking the entrance. "You can't go in there. This is a crime scene."

Clay tries to shoulder past me. I plant my feet and shove back harder.

"This is a crime scene, Clay," I repeat, firmer this time. "We can't risk contamination."

Boone lays a steadying hand on his shoulder. "I know this is hard, son. But she's right. We don't want to compromise the evidence."

Clay's jaw works. He bites down on his trembling lip as he peers over my shoulder, inside the boathouse. "That's her. I recognize the pink sports bra."

He drags his eyes away, takes a shuddering breath, then turns back to me. "How'd you find her?"

"Dad was here fishing. I stopped by to see what he caught."

Clay's gaze shifts, narrowing as he notices Dad for the first time. "Fishing? Or missing?"

The hair on my neck prickles. "Fishing," I say evenly. "He left his phone at home. I came down to ask if he needed anything from the store." A version of the truth—but the truth, nonetheless.

"Mm-hmm," Clay mutters. "The killer returns to the scene."

He says it under his breath, but I catch it, and I know exactly where he's aiming. He's going to pin this on Dad. Yesterday, he liked *some sick bastard* for the crime. But this is better, more believable—the old man with the fading memory.

Clay pivots toward him. "Where were you Thursday night, Judge Sutherlin?"

The color drains from Dad's face. His mouth opens, but no words come out.

"He was home," I snap, looking to Boone for backup. "You spoke to him when you stopped by looking for Addie."

The sheriff gives a slow nod. "That's right."

Clay takes a step closer, looming over Dad, towering like a predator scenting weakness—one young, strong man against another old and fading one. "That was after eleven. Where were you before?"

Dad drops his chin, eyes fixed on the rotting planks. His voice is barely audible. "I'm not sure."

Boone clears his throat, shifting the focus. "What happened here?" He crouches, studying the splintered wood around the knob.

"Scout was pawing at the door," I say. "She must've smelled Addie inside. The door was locked, so I kicked it in."

"Where is Scout now?" the sheriff asks.

"I couldn't control her, so I put her in the car." I glance toward the SUV, the windows fogged from her frantic panting. Part of me wants to let her out, see how she reacts to Clay. Dogs know things people don't. But she'll try to get to Addie again, and I can't bear to watch.

More crunch on gravel announces the arrival of the crime scene van. The white door slides open, and techs in gloves and booties head for the boathouse, evidence kits in hand.

Boone takes charge with the authority of a man who's done this many times. "Secure the perimeter. Photograph the entry. No one touches her until we've documented."

Boone ducks inside, careful not to disturb the splintered door-frame, and kneels beside the body. I hover at the threshold, straining to hear. His voice is low, clinical, each word clipped as he points out the faint abrasions circling her throat—the telltale ligature marks. Then his tone falters.

"Damn, Addie," he mutters, swiping at his eyes before standing.

His words gut me. Boone's seen plenty of bodies—but not our sweet Addie. A tremor runs through me, but I lock it down, unwilling to let Clay see me break.

While Boone is busy, Clay seizes his chance. He sidles up to

Dad, voice low but sharp as a blade. "So you left your phone at home, did you? Folks say you've been having a rough time—wandering off, forgetting things. Word around town is dementia." His gaze hardens, merciless. "For all we know, you killed her and don't even remember it."

Anger scorches through me, fast and hot. "Shut up, Clay! You're way out of line."

He spins toward me, jaw locked. "*You* shut up, Lane. Your father may have killed my wife."

The air detonates. Voices rise, fury collides. My pulse hammers so loud I can't hear myself think—until Boone storms out of the boathouse and wedges himself between us.

"That's enough!" His voice cuts through the chaos like a gavel strike. "What's wrong with y'all? Keep your voices down—this is a crime scene, not a bar fight."

Clay jabs a finger at Dad, eyes blazing. "Come on, Sheriff. You know that man is not in his right mind. It's too much of a coincidence that he just happened to be fishing outside the boathouse where my dead wife was found. He's hiding something. And he doesn't even know what he's hiding."

A look of disgust flickers across Boone's face. "I agree with Lane. You're way out of line, Dalton. I've known Hollis Sutherlin most of my life. He wouldn't hurt a flea."

Clay doesn't flinch. "With all due respect, sir, dementia changes people. Strips them of their dignity. Twists them into someone else entirely."

Boone casts Hollis a sympathetic glance before turning back to Clay. "I have seen nothing that makes me doubt his judgment. Not yet."

While they tear apart his character like he's invisible, I grip Dad's arm and pull him aside. My voice drops, low and urgent. "This is serious, Dad. Clay will not let this go. You need to remember where you were on Thursday night. Even saying you were alone is better than admitting you don't remember."

His face is blank. He doesn't have a clue.

"Try, Dad. Did Judd come over? Did you see anyone? Dinner with friends?"

Then, like a match catching, his hazel eyes brighten. "That's it. I had dinner with the McCrays. Doris and Evan invited me over. We sat on the porch. Evan grilled ribs. They were delicious."

Relief floods me. Not only is Evan McCray an old friend, he's a criminal attorney with an untarnished reputation. If anyone can vouch for Dad, he can.

"Mystery solved," I announce, rejoining the others. "Dad had dinner Thursday night with Doris and Evan McCray."

Clay's face tightens. "We need to confirm that. Call Evan."

Boone pulls out his phone and clicks on the number.

"On speaker," Clay demands.

Boone obliges. The line rings, and Evan's deep voice fills the air. "Afternoon, Boone. What can I do for you?"

"I need you to clear up a little misunderstanding," Boone says. "Can you confirm Hollis had dinner with you on Thursday night?"

A pause. "Why? Is something wrong?"

"This is an ongoing investigation. I can't divulge any details. I just need you to verify Hollis's whereabouts on Thursday night."

"I see." Another pause, heavier this time. "We had Hollis over recently, but it was several weeks ago."

Boone's eyes narrow. "You're sure it wasn't Thursday?"

"I'm positive. If Hollis is in trouble, tell him I'll help however I can."

"Thanks. We'll get back to you if we need you," Sheriff says, ending the call.

Boone slips the phone back into his pocket. For a long moment, no one says a word.

Then, Clay's lips curve into a grim smile. "Well, isn't that convenient? First, he doesn't remember, then he lies about his whereabouts."

I feel Dad sway beside me, his shoulders caving inward, his confidence deflating as quickly as it came. He looks like a man untethered, one who knows the ground beneath him has just given way.

"Dad," I whisper, desperate. "Think again. Where were you on Thursday? Night before last."

But his eyes are glassy, far away. He doesn't answer.

Clay spreads his arms wide, as if the answer is in the air. "You heard it yourselves. He doesn't remember. He *can't* remember. Tell me, Sheriff—how much more probable cause do you need?"

Boone doesn't answer right away. His eyes dart between Clay, Dad, and me. For the first time, I see hesitation in his face.

And just like that, this nightmare takes on new teeth.

"Book him, Sheriff. For the murder of my wife." Clay grabs for his cuffs.

Boone's hand shoots up. "Hold your horses, Clay. You're too close to this situation. Back off and let me handle it."

Clay bristles, ready to argue, but Boone's glare shuts him down. With a huff, he stalks off, muttering under his breath.

My chest tightens, and I feel panic rising like bile. "Sheriff, you're not seriously going to arrest him." Dad can't survive this— not the shame, not the confusion.

Boone sighs, rubbing the back of his neck. "Honestly, he'll be safer in custody until we can sort this out. It'll keep him out of Clay's crosshairs and away from town gossip." He turns to Dad, laying a steady hand on his arm. "Hollis Sutherlin, I'm taking you into custody on suspicion of murder."

The words clang in my ears, impossible to absorb. My chest seizes, panic rising like bile. "Sheriff, you can't do this," I plead, hurrying at their side as Boone guides Dad toward his car.

"I have no choice, Lane."

"How long before the magistrate arraigns him?"

"Monday morning. He's out of town at his son's wedding." Boone opens the back door and helps Dad inside with surprising gentleness.

"*Monday morning*? You've gotta be kidding me. What kind of operation are you running?"

"Small town, Lane. That's the way it is."

Dread grips me like a vise. "What can I do? How can I help? Can I at least bring him some clothes—his pajamas, his toothbrush?"

Boone nods. "You can do that. But if you really wanna help?" His eyes lock on mine, hard now. "Figure out where your daddy was Thursday night."

"Damn right, I will."

Clay may think he's found his scapegoat, but the blame won't stick. Not if I have anything to do with it.

Chapter Ten

I follow the sheriff at a safe distance down the gravel road toward the entrance to the park. Through the rear window, I glimpse Dad's head bobbing, animated as he gives Boone an earful. He's himself again. At least for the moment.

When the patrol car turns toward town, I peel off in the opposite direction toward the farm. Pulling up in front of the house, I kill the engine and press my forehead against the steering wheel. I'm usually sharp in a crisis, with blood pumping and adrenaline rushing to keep my head clear. But this is different. My best friend is dead, and my father has been accused of killing her. The shock has fractured my thoughts into sharp little pieces I can't line up.

One task at a time, I tell myself. First, take Dad some clothes. Then find a way to get the charges dropped. After that, hunt down Addie's real killer. I can't afford to let my emotions cloud my judgment. Grieving will have to wait until this is over.

Upstairs, I pull Dad's overnight carry-on from the hall closet and neatly pack several changes of clothes, his pajamas, robe, and slippers. In the bathroom, I toss in his toiletries and blood pressure medicine. Every fold, every zip steadies me, a rhythm for my hands when my heart can't find one.

When I come back downstairs, Scout is planted at the door,

muscles taut, ears pricked, like she's bracing for battle. Who knows what's spinning through her head. Outside, when I open the car door, she doesn't bound into the front seat like usual. She curls into a tight ball in the back, nose to the window, shutting out the world.

Scout shutting herself off feels like a warning, and I can't shake it. My next stop is the sheriff's department, a place I've avoided since the night Boone saved me—the night my life split in two.

I breeze past the front desk, muttering that I'm here to see Sheriff Boone, not slowing when the attendant calls for me to wait. Even after all this time, I remember the way to his office.

Boone is tilted back in his chair, eyes closed, boots propped on desk, his face carved in a tight expression of exhaustion and worry. I drop Dad's suitcase by the door with a loud thud. He springs upright, the chair skidding a few inches before bumping the desk.

"Geez, Lane! You scared me to death." He snatches his reading glasses from the blotter and peers at me over the rims.

"Can I see him?"

"Not right now. We're processing him."

Processing. The word lands like a slap. Fingerprints. Mug shot. My proud, addled father humiliated under fluorescent lights. The Honorable Judge Sutherlin reduced to an inmate.

"Deputize me, Sheriff." My voice comes out sharp, demanding.

His brows lift, gray and bushy, as he studies me. "I've got plenty of deputies, Lane."

"But you don't have any investigators. I can do what your deputies can't." I step closer, my pulse drumming in my ears. "I'm working the case—with or without your blessing. You don't have to pay me, but I'll be more effective with your resources."

He pushes back from his desk, the chair creaking under his weight as he stands. "I've followed your career, Lane. You've made a name for yourself in Richmond. Folks here are proud of you, whether or not you know it. Your reputation precedes you."

For a second, I think he's about to hand me a badge on the spot. Then his tone hardens.

"But I've also seen what happens when people get too close. You're not just an investigator—you're the judge's daughter, *the accused's* daughter. And Addie, *the victim,* was your best friend. Not only is that a conflict of interest, it's a dangerous mix. Grief makes a lousy partner in an investigation."

The words are on my tongue—*Isn't Clay working his wife's murder a conflict of interest?* But I hold them back. Making the sheriff angry won't get me what I want.

"I don't need a partner, Sheriff. I need access. Badge, files, whatever you've got. Like it or not, I'm already in this."

He studies me for a long moment, the silence as heavy as the tide before a storm. "That fire in you—it's what makes you good. But it's also what can get you burned."

"I'll take that risk," I say, squaring my shoulders. "For Addie. For Dad. For the truth."

Boone exhales slowly, rubbing his temple. "All right. But only because I can see there's nothing stopping you. You're walking a fine line between justice and vengeance, Lane. Be careful which side you land on."

"Yes, sir. Thank you, sir."

Boone opens his top desk drawer, rummaging until he finds a tarnished badge. He turns it over in his hand before sliding it across the desk to me.

"Don't make me regret this. You get the badge. Not the gun. Not yet. I want you reporting straight to me, Lane. No detours, no grandstanding."

I close my fingers around the cool metal, my pulse thrumming. "Understood."

"Good! Now, get out of my office. I have work to do."

When he gestures at the door, I don't move.

"Is there something else, Lane?"

"About Dad . . . I'm afraid to leave him here alone. He's not himself these days."

Boone's shoulders sag. "No, he's not. And it breaks my heart." He comes around to my side of the desk, looming close enough that I catch the faint scent of his woodsy aftershave. "Don't worry, Lane. He's in good hands. We've already made a date to play cards later, and Betty is bringing his favorite chicken potpie."

Relief softens my chest. "But what if he wakes up confused? Doesn't know where he is?"

"I'll make sure the guards are aware of his challenges. At least in here we can keep an eye on him—better than him wandering around the farm at night."

"That's true. We have some things to figure out, but I'm on it, sir."

He wags a finger at me. "And stop calling me *sir*. I changed your diapers when you were a baby."

My eyes widen. "Seriously?"

Boone chuckles. "Heck, no. Betty never let me near our own kids' diapers. But I remember the day you were born."

A mischievous smile tugs at my lips. "So? Should I call you Uncle Franklin?"

He tilts his head, considering. "Could. But then folks would accuse us of favoritism. Better stick with Boone or Sheriff like everyone else."

His hand squeezes my arm, his voice dropping low. "Your daddy loves you, Lane. Always called you his peach. I can't imagine how hard this is for you. Not because of the arrest—we both know he didn't kill Addie. But the dementia . . . that's a terrible disease."

"No one told me," I whisper. "I figured it out once I got here."

"Well, now . . . ain't that just a crying shame. You once had a beautiful family . . ."

His voice trails off, but I know what he's thinking. Families don't always recover from trauma.

Boone bends to pat Scout's head. "If only this dog could talk."

"Right? She knows everything. When the time comes, she'll tell us in her own way."

I head for the door. "Keep an eye on Dad for me. Let me know if he needs anything. In the meantime, I'm going to catch a killer."

Boone's laughter follows me down the hall, but with every step away from Dad, the knife in my chest drives in a little deeper.

I'm easing out of the parking lot when Scout growls—low and guttural. Her hackles rise, eyes fixed on something outside.

I follow her gaze. Clay.

He strides into my path and slams a fist against the hood.

I roll down the window halfway. "Move."

He leans in close. His breath is hot and sour—too much coffee, not enough water. "Your daddy—the *Honorable* Judge Hollis Sutherlin—killed my wife. And he's going to rot in prison for the rest of his short, miserable life."

"Dad didn't kill Addie. And I aim to prove it." I hold up my badge so it glints in the sunlight. "Meet your new criminal investigator. Which means I outrank you. So *move*."

"Big-city detective." Clay's sneer deepens. "You won't last a day here, Sutherlin. Badge or not, you're still a nobody in this town."

I give him a slow, dry smile. "You talk big for someone who reeks of dead fish and poor decisions. Better work on your alibi— because I'm coming for you."

Scout explodes against the glass, barking until the Bronco rattles.

Clay doesn't flinch. He just smiles—slow and cold.

I slam the Bronco into gear. He steps back, still smiling.

<h1 style="text-align:center">Chapter Eleven</h1>

I'm flying down Tidewater Drive, blind to the speed limit, when Judd's name lights up my dash. A groan escapes me, sharp enough that Scout lifts her head from the backseat.

I search for her brown eyes in the rearview mirror. "Nothing for you to worry about, girl. It's just my brother."

I stab the Bluetooth button on the steering wheel, forcing calm into my voice. "What's up?" The last thing I need is Judd sniffing out my frayed nerves.

But his voice is tight, edged with something close to panic. "Is it true?" He doesn't wait for me to answer. "Did they arrest Dad—for Addie's murder?"

My chest squeezes. "Yep, it's true. Boone's taking care of him, but it doesn't look good."

The line goes quiet. I can hear Judd breathing, processing. "Where are you now?"

"On my way home."

"I'll meet you there in a few," he says, ending the call.

I pull into the driveway ahead of him, slip through the mudroom, and set out a bowl of water for Scout. The house feels too still, too quiet—like it's holding its breath.

Five minutes later, the door bursts open. Judd barrels in, his voice already raised. "I swear, Lane, you drag trouble with you everywhere you go."

I snap upright, hand slicing the air. "Don't you dare blame me for this. If you'd told me about Dad's dementia, maybe we wouldn't be in this mess. Instead, you've been letting him wander the countryside unchaperoned."

Judd bristles. "You think it's that easy? You think I can just chain him to the porch? I'd like to see you do better."

"Maybe I can't. But I deserve the chance to try." My voice cracks, anger giving way to something more fragile. "Why did you keep this from me, Judd?"

"If I'd told you, would you have come home?"

I can't answer. After the divorce . . . after everything else this year, I don't know if I would have.

"That's what I thought." His shoulders sag, but his eyes stay hard. "I've been doing my best, but taking care of him is a full-time job." He jabs a finger into my chest. "You're staying here now. Where were *you* today when he was wandering around the park, lost?"

"He wasn't lost. He was fishing. Last night at dinner, he told me he wanted to go to the Tide House. That's how I knew where to look for him." My throat thickens. "As for my whereabouts earlier today, I was trying to find Addie, my missing best friend. Mission accomplished."

Judd drops onto a barstool, the fight draining out of him. "I'm sorry about Addie. She was a good girl. She didn't deserve this."

I ease onto the stool beside him. "No, she didn't."

"Tell me how Dad got caught up in this mess."

So I do—Clay pointing the finger at Dad, Boone having no choice but to arrest him, Dad driving away in the back of the sheriff's cruiser—every detail until my throat feels scraped raw.

"When's the arraignment?" he asks.

"Not until Monday. The magistrate is out of town. Which gives me twenty-four hours to find an alibi. Any clue what Dad did Thursday night?"

"None. I try to call him most nights, but Brandy and I went out to dinner with friends on Thursday. We didn't get back until late. I figured he was asleep." Judd buries his face in his hands. "This is all my fault. I knew something was wrong with him. I just didn't want to face it. Admitting it meant everything would change. And I wasn't ready for that. I'm still not ready for it."

I think about what Judd said the other night. *He's still fine. He hasn't gotten lost driving. Pays his bills. Knows my name.* Denial dressed up as reassurance.

"We don't have the luxury of pretending anymore. He's being charged with suspicion of murder because he can't remember where he was at the time of the crime. It doesn't get much worse than that. But we'll get through it, Judd. As long as we stick together."

"I'm so sorry, Lane. What do you want from me?" His voice cracks, the anger gone, leaving only exhaustion.

Boone's words echo in my head. *Well, now . . . ain't that just a crying shame. You once had a beautiful family.* Judd and I are all that's left of our family. Hollis has been a strong, loyal father. We owe it to him to do right by him.

I get up to make Scout a peanut butter snack. "It's a lot to handle, but we're in this together. You and I both have busy lives. It's not our job to babysit Dad. But it's our responsibility to find someone who can."

His gaze lifts. "Someone's gotta manage those someones. Which means me—since you skipped out on this family."

Ouch. His words slice clean through me. I want to argue, to remind him I've built a life of my own. But the truth is that life is already unraveling. No matter how many caregivers we hire, no matter how many schedules we shuffle, Dad's decline will bleed into everything. Piece by piece, he's slipping away—and we'll both be pulled under with him.

I remember Judd mentioning memory care the other night.

The thought of putting Dad in a place like that makes me cringe. "If we put our heads together, we can figure this out. Lally comes every weekday. Maybe she can stay a little later—feed him dinner, get him into bed."

Judd glares at me as though I've grown a second head. "Lally? Have you seen her lately?" He palms his head. "What am I thinking? You haven't been home. You don't know. Lally's getting old, Lane. I'm not sure how much longer she'll be able to work for us."

"Oh." My heart sinks at the thought of Lally—our long-time housekeeper, the woman who sneaked me sugar cookies after school—getting old. "We should at least ask her if she knows where Dad was on Thursday night. Maybe he mentioned dinner with friends. Can you imagine not being able to remember where you were?"

He shakes his head, a little shiver rippling through him. Then his eyes harden. "No. But if we don't figure out where he was, he'll be in prison, and we won't have to worry about his dementia." He exhales a frustrated breath, the words sounding harsher than he means them. "The reality is, Dad was probably here alone on Thursday night. How are we gonna prove that?"

"Let's exhaust his other options first."

He cuts his eyes at me. "How do you suggest we do that?"

I shrug, feeling the weight of it all. "Call everyone Dad knows, I guess."

Judd swings his legs around and hops off the stool. "We can divide and conquer." He disappears down the hall, returning with Dad's leather address book—the same one he's kept since I was a kid, pages worn soft from decades of phone calls.

We take turns calling his local friends, treading carefully, trying not to sound desperate. Most have already heard about his arrest. While none can recall his whereabouts on Thursday night, all are sympathetic and supportive. The kindhearted Hollis Sutherlin wouldn't hurt a living soul.

It grows dark, and our stomachs grumble. Judd orders a pizza while I run to the cottage for Scout's food. We eat outside on the terrace, the sinking sun painting the sky in shades of pink and orange.

"Do you see Mom much?" I ask, peeling off a slice of pepperoni.

"Hardly ever. Most of the time, she ignores me when I run into her in town. She's got her nose stuck so far up her stepdaughters' butts, she's totally forgotten about you and me."

I shake my head in bewilderment. "I don't get it. What did we ever do to her?"

"That's the way she is, Laney. She uses people." He tosses a piece of crust into the box. "Dad was too upstanding for her, too by-the-book and old school. He couldn't give her the glitzy life she thinks she deserves, so she found herself a new sugar daddy. Funny thing is, her stepdaughters make fun of her behind her back. The truth? Mom is the laughingstock of the town."

"Really? I always thought they divorced because of . . . you know, Tommy."

A faraway look settles over his face. "There's so much you don't know about our family. About the accident."

I stiffen, heart thudding. I always suspected more to the story. "Tell me."

He hesitates. For a second, I think he's about to open the door to our deepest family secrets—then he shrugs it off. "Nah. You're better off not knowing. You can't change the past."

Disappointment presses in, sharp and familiar. All my life, I've circled the edges of that night, waiting for someone to peel back the curtain. But maybe some doors stay locked for a reason.

"How are things with Brandy? You two getting along okay?"

He grabs another slice of pizza and falls back in his chair. "Mostly. We're trying for a baby."

"I was wondering about that. You've been married for a while now."

He rolls his eyes. "Tell me about it. Every month she doesn't get pregnant, she turns into a she-devil. Blames me. But I've been tested. The problem ain't me. I'm firing live rounds."

I laugh him off, but the sound feels hollow in my throat. Between Addie's death, Dad's arrest, and Judd's unfinished confession, I can't shake the sense that shadows are closing in on us from every direction. And sooner or later, one of them is bound to swallow us whole.

Chapter Twelve

I wait until after noon on Sunday to visit Lally. Even though I haven't been there in decades, I remember exactly how to get to Captain's Row—the historic waterfront neighborhood several miles past the Oyster Bay resort. A quiet pocket along the river's curve, Captain's Row was first settled in 1706 by families drawn to the waterfront and the promise of new beginnings. The streets are narrow and shaded, lined with weathered oaks and old cottages that lean with the years—homes built by the watermen and shipwrights who carved out this town long before the resort crowd arrived. A few have been restored with glossy paint and wraparound porches, but most still wear their age honestly— peeling clapboard, slanted roofs, and gardens bursting with marigolds and mint.

When my parents were away on one of their many trips, Lally used to bring us here—Tommy, Judd, and me piled into the back of Mama's station wagon—so she could check on her own children. I hated when my parents were away, and it made me sad she had to choose us over them.

Lally's home is small but tidy—blue shutters, pansies along the sidewalk, mums in planters on the porch. She answers the door still dressed from church—a bright yellow hat to match her sunny suit. Judd was right. She has aged—her shoulders stooped, hair gone gray—but her warm brown eyes are kind, and her smile is as radiant as ever.

She seems relieved to see me. "Lord, child, I'm so worried about the judge." She engulfs me in a hug. "Hardly anyone at church could talk about anything else. Your daddy always treated me—and our folks—with kindness and respect. And people don't forget that kind of decency. Half the congregation wanted to march down to that jail."

"Thank you for saying that, Lally. It means a lot." I blink back tears. For someone who never cries, I've been on the verge of a meltdown these past few days.

She gestures to the pair of rockers. "Can I get you some sweet tea?"

"No, thanks. I can only stay a minute." I lower myself to a chair, and she settles in beside me, the boards creaking softly beside us.

"When did you get to town? I figured you'd come once you heard Addie was missing. Sweet child. I always loved her so," Lally says, dabbing at her eyes with a lace handkerchief.

I smile faintly. "She was special. I can hardly believe she's gone." The smile fades. "I got in around lunchtime on Friday. I'm surprised you weren't there."

"I took the day off to drive up to Richmond for a doctor's appointment."

I frown. "Nothing serious, I hope."

"Just my old heart. Gets out of whack from time to time. The doctor adjusted my medication." She pats her chest. "She's ticking better now."

"Good. With everything going on with Dad, we can't afford for anything to happen to you." I shift in my chair, angling my body toward her. "Speaking of Dad, I'm hoping you can shed some light on his whereabouts on Thursday night."

"I wish I could, Laney girl. I've been wracking my brain, but I can't think of anything out of the ordinary. He didn't mention having dinner with friends. I noticed there wasn't much food in the house, so I offered to go to the market. But he waved me off, said he'd rustle something up. When I left the house around five o'clock, he was snoozing in the leather chair in his study."

"Judd never bothered telling me about his memory slipping. His empty fridge was the first clue that something was off."

Lally's face tightens, her disapproval clear. I'm sure she's held plenty of opinions about my family over the years, though she respects us too much to voice them. "I'm sure Judd didn't want to worry you."

"Dad is going to need more help, Lally. Do you have any thoughts on how we can manage that?"

She taps her chin. "I'm already running errands for him— picking up groceries, the dry-cleaning, prescriptions. I can do more of that if need be. I leave him dinner sometimes. He complains about the fuss, but I do it anyway. I can do that every night if you think it'd help."

"That would be wonderful, Lally. At least make sure he gets dinner." I rest my head on the back of the chair. "I was actually thinking more along the lines of caregivers. Someone around to make sure he doesn't wander off."

Lally clucks her tongue. "Your daddy won't like that. He'll see it as losing his independence. But I understand. It's a necessary evil if it keeps him safe."

"To keep him safe *and* at home. He's still so young. I'd hate to put him in a nursing home."

"Lord, help us. Don't do that." She shakes her head, genuine distress flickering across her face. Then she brightens a little. "My niece runs a private care company. She hires certified nursing assistants—not full nurses, but well-trained and capable."

I sit up straighter. "That's exactly what we need. Please share her contact information."

She nods firmly. "I'll let Hannah know you'll be reaching out."

We talk for a few minutes about Addie, reliving the happy days of our youth—our innocent shenanigans and adventures.

When I stand to leave, Lally grips my shoulders. "I love you, Laney girl, like one of my own. Your family means the world to me. If you need anything, don't hesitate to ask."

The drive back to town feels quieter than before, the weight of everything pressing on my chest. On impulse, I turn onto Bayview Drive and stop at the spot where I found Scout. When I let her out of the car, she recognizes the place right away—nose to the ground, snuffling across the gravel, then deeper into the reeds at the marsh's edge. I crouch beside her, following her lead, not sure what I'm hoping to find but desperate for something.

Her phone would be a gold mine. Unfortunately, it's probably long gone. Still, I make a mental note to have Boone subpoena the carrier for Addie's text-message log. Just in case. I plan to have this solved before the paperwork clears.

I'm crawling on all fours when I spot it—a faint glimmer in the mud. Reaching for it, I lift a tiny gold wedding band out of the mud. It's simple and delicate—made for a woman's finger. *Addie's* finger.

But where's her engagement ring? The stunning solitaire diamond that belonged to Clay's grandmother that Addie was so proud of. Becoming a Dalton had been a kind of arrival for her. After years of scraping by, she finally felt seen. She used to joke that marrying Clay was like stepping through the gates of Tidewell's country club and never having to leave.

I press the band into my palm, mud squelching between my fingers. All that glitter and promise stripped down to this—one plain gold circle sinking into the marsh.

Stuffing the band into my pocket, I dig frantically, sinking my hands into the muck. Scout joins me, pawing at the earth as if she could dig up Addie herself. Tears blur my vision, and I collapse, clutching the dog against me, her muddy fur smearing my clothes.

"She's not coming back, sweet girl," I whisper into her neck. "She's gone for good. It's just you and me now. But I promise I'll take good care of you. Always."

I don't even know if my Richmond apartment allows dogs—but it doesn't matter. The thought feels distant, belonging to another life. I'm beginning to accept what I already know deep down. I won't be going back there. Not to that life. My father's failing health will keep me in Tidewell.

And the funny thing is—I'm not sure I mind.

Determination burns hotter in my chest as I lead Scout back to the car. *I will find who killed my best friend if it's the last thing I do.*

I drive across the road to Patriots Landing Marina. Parking beside the office, I head inside with Scout at my heels. Behind the counter stands a young man with stringy brown hair and a pock-marked face.

"I'm Detective Lane Sutherlin, working with the sheriff's department. I need your surveillance footage from Thursday night."

He gives me a long, doubtful once-over. I'm a mess with mud-streaked clothes, puffy eyes, hair like a rat's nest.

I flash him my badge. "This is about Addie Dalton's murder. I believe she may have been killed nearby."

His suspicion shifts to surprise. "Right. I heard about that. But I don't have access to the cameras. The app is on my boss's phone, and he's fishing in Costa Rica."

"When do you expect him back?"

The guy shrugs. "End of next week. Maybe later. I'm not really sure."

"You have no way of reaching him?"

"I can try, but he's probably out of cell range."

"Try anyway. This is important. Let me know if you find out anything." I scribble my name and number on a scrap of paper and slide it across the counter.

"Will do," he says.

I step away, muttering to Scout, "Looks like we're pulling a stakeout." Her ears perk as if she approves. "First stop—snacks."

From the marina's tiny grocery corner, I fill a basket with popcorn, peanuts, dog treats, and bottled water.

Outside, I move the Bronco to the far edge of the lot and roll down my window for a clearer view of my surroundings. The marina stretches into Oyster Bay in neat rows of rocking boats, masts clicking like wind chimes in the breeze. Scout settles into the passenger seat, chin propped on the window ledge, her breath fogging the glass. The water lies still in the fading light, disturbed only by gulls skimming low and the lazy ripple of a passing skiff.

I crunch peanuts, eyes sweeping the marina, as the next hour crawls by. Nothing happens—just the usual ebb and flow of boat owners tinkering on their decks, hauling coolers down the docks, laughing at conversations I can't hear.

Then movement catches my eye—a tall man with dark hair wrestling grocery bags from the back of his pickup. Even from the distance, I know that lanky frame—Ben Holloway.

Scout lets out a low whine, ears pricked, tail thumping against the seat.

"Yeah, I see him too," I murmur, pressing a hand to her back. I remember how she leaped into his lap yesterday at Slip 99, covering his face with licks. Ben is more to Scout than someone she passes on a walk.

My stomach tightens as I watch him stride down the dock toward an old houseboat, the grocery bags swinging against his legs.

Does Ben live here? Is that his boat? I'm not surprised. His legs were always steadier on water than on land.

Addie and Scout were near here on Thursday night—the night she went missing. Is it just a coincidence? In Tidewell, everyone knows everyone, and plenty of folks live on boats. Still, unease prickles under my skin as the houseboat door shuts behind him, leaving only the creak of the dock and the soft slap of water against the pilings.

Chapter Thirteen

I'm late leaving for court on Monday morning, and by the time I slip into the front row, the courtroom is already packed. Neighbors. Church friends. Old colleagues from the bar association. They've all come to stand behind my father—Tidewell's beloved judge.

For thirty years, they trusted him to hand down justice. Today, they're here to return the favor, a wall of loyalty against the ugly rumor that he killed a young woman. Their presence steadies me until I look up at the bench. Judge Vernon Tate—his black robe straining across his belly, the fabric shiny where it's rubbed thin. That crooked toupee still sits like a dead squirrel on his head. I've never liked him. I have no valid reason—just instinct. Something about him has always rubbed me wrong.

I lean across the railing toward Evan McCray—Dad's attorney. "Why is Tate presiding?" I ask in a loud whisper. "Where's the magistrate?"

"Travel delays," he mutters. "Tate offered to step in."

"Of course he did," I say under my breath. Tate never shies away from the spotlight.

A hush settles over the crowd when the door opens, and a deputy escorts my father inside. Gasps ripple through the gallery, followed by a low roar of whispers at the sight of his hands cuffed and his feet shackled. His bewildered expression—the look of a man who's wandered into the wrong house—shatters my heart into a million pieces. He has no idea what's happening.

"Seriously, Evan? Shackles? What the hell is going on?"

Evan covers his mouth with his hand, voice low. "I'm not sure. The sheriff would never allow it."

I scan the deputies. No Boone. Just Clay, proud as a rooster. "Where is Boone anyway?"

"Good question."

As Dad approaches, Evan pulls out his chair and gives his shoulder a squeeze, whispering something that earns a faint, confused smile.

Tate cracks his gavel. "Court is now in session." His voice booms, silencing the murmurs. "Commonwealth versus Hollis Monroe Sutherlin." His oily smile sweeps the room. "Mr. Briggs, you may proceed."

A young man in a tailored navy suit rises at the prosecution's table. Sun-streaked hair, lean frame—the sort of man who makes people notice without trying. "Thank you, Your Honor." His easy Southern drawl rolls across the room, and every woman on the front row sits up straighter.

Great! Just what I need. A prosecutor who looks like Matthew McConaughey.

Then it clicks. I know him. Lawson Briggs. Tommy's best friend. I haven't seen him since the funeral. As a young teenager, I had the biggest crush on him, despite the four years between us. He probably knew it—I wasn't exactly subtle—but he never teased me about it. He always treated me with kindness, like the kid sister he never had.

I always pictured him as a politician—always smiling, always scheming. But here he is—the commonwealth's attorney, a prosecutor. I can't help but wonder what might've come of Tommy if he'd been given the chance. Of the three of us, Tommy was the most likely to follow Dad into law. His sharp mind and intuition would've served him well. Could he have carried on the Sutherlin legacy?

Briggs clears his throat, squaring his shoulders toward the bench. When he speaks, his tone is confident and controlled. "New evidence has come to light, Your Honor. An eyewitness places a man matching Hollis Sutherlin's description near the boathouse on the night of Addie Dalton's death."

Gasps ripple through the courtroom. My stomach flips. I grip the edge of the bench so hard my knuckles ache. "That's impossible," I whisper—more to myself than anyone else. But in Dad's state of mind, I can't be sure.

Evan's jaw tightens. He leans toward Dad, but his voice carries. "It's a setup. Boone would've told us." Then he straightens and addresses the judge. "Your Honor, the commonwealth makes a grave allegation. Who is this so-called eyewitness? We demand disclosure."

"All in due course, Mr. McCray." Tate's gavel taps once, more for show than order.

I shake my head, not believing this. Boone should've disclosed this witness to the defense, not ambushed us in court.

Tate's gaze slides to the prosecutor. "The court finds probable cause. Please proceed, Mr. Briggs."

Briggs slowly stands. "Your Honor, the commonwealth formally charges Hollis Monroe Sutherlin with second-degree murder. Given the seriousness of the offense and the eyewitness placing the defendant at the scene, we recommend bail be set at five hundred thousand dollars.

Evan's chair scrapes the floor as he shoots to his feet. "Your Honor, that bail amount is ludicrous. My client is not a flight risk. He's a well-respected retired judge with deep roots in this community."

Tate glares at him. "Mr. McCray, the court has been made aware of the defendant's cognitive decline, which raises concerns about his ability to comply with conditions of release. Given the gravity of the charge and the uncertainty of his mental state, bail is set at one million dollars. Preliminary hearing is set for two weeks from today."

The courtroom erupts. Evan raises his voice over the noise. "But Your Honor, that's outrageous! There's been no medical evaluation entered into evidence, no hearing, no testimony of any kind regarding Judge Sutherlin's health. You're making assumptions not supported by the record."

Tate lifts a hand, palm out, like he's swatting a fly. "Sit down, Mr. McCray. The court has ruled."

"With respect, sir, this isn't a ruling—it's punishment before trial."

The judge's eyes narrow. "Watch yourself, Counselor."

Evan draws a breath, visibly reining it in. "Then at least permit me to request a bail review hearing."

"Denied," Tate snaps. "We're done here."

His gavel slams down again, louder this time, and the sound rings through the courtroom like a gunshot.

I reach for Dad as the deputy takes his arm, guiding him to stand. His cuffed hands tremble as he turns to look for me, eyes clouded and confused.

"Don't worry, Dad. I'll talk to Mr. Carroway. We'll raise the money for the bondsman."

Dad shakes his head, grave and weary. "There's no money to raise, Laney Bug."

Behind me, a woman's voice hitches. I turn to find several locals watching me, pity etched across their faces. The rumors will spread like wildfire—the judge has no money.

As the deputy leads him away, he glances back over his shoulder. "Don't worry. I'll be fine. Boone will look after me in jail."

Grabbing my belongings, I hurry after him, but by the time I reach the hallway, he's gone. A confused-looking Boone spots me and pulls me aside, out of the stream of people spilling out of the courtroom.

"What on earth happened in there? Why is everyone in such an uproar?"

"Where have you been, Sheriff? That's the bigger question."

"I got a call about a missing kid," Boone says, rubbing the back of his neck. "The woman was hysterical. She claimed her baby had been snatched from her crib. She called me directly—never said how she got my number. I had no choice but to investigate."

"And?"

"Nothing. The address was bogus. The road exists, but the house doesn't. I drove the whole stretch twice before I figured it out. Damnedest thing."

I study his face. Boone's too good at his job to be chasing ghosts. Somebody wanted him out of that courtroom. The thought lands heavy in my gut, though I can't yet prove it. But when I picture Clay's smug smile as Dad shuffled in wearing shackles, I know one thing for certain—none of this was an accident.

Clay is playing chess, not checkers.

"Do you know about this so-called witness who claims they saw Dad near the boathouse on Thursday night?" I ask, watching for his reaction.

His brows shoot up toward his thinning hairline. "What eyewitness?"

"You tell me—you're the sheriff." When I fill him in about the murder-two charge and million-dollar bail, his face flushes red—the color of a cherry popsicle.

"If you ask me, someone set you up. Lured you out of the courtroom so you wouldn't raise hell about the bail, so you wouldn't push for Dad to be released on his own recognizance."

"That's a stretch, Lane."

I shrug. "Maybe so. To make matters worse, Dad swears he doesn't have the money for the bondsman."

Boone lowers his head, his voice softer. "That may be true, Lane. But talk to Charlie Carroway. He handles all of Hollis's finances. He can give you a clearer picture. In the meantime, I'm looking out for your daddy. He's safe with me."

I lean in, my words sharp. "Don't be so sure. Whoever is

guarding him, you'd better trust them with your life. Because someone is out to get him. You and I both know who that is."

"Who?"

"Clay Dalton."

Boone shakes his head, almost smiling in disbelief. "Nah. Not Clay."

Of course. The sheriff's like every other sucker in this town—a victim of the charming Prince of Tidewell. He'll find out soon enough. I just hope it's not at my father's expense.

Chapter Fourteen

B ack at the farm, I brew a cup of coffee and take it out to the porch. Scout crawls under the table, her tail thumping softly against the brick as I flip through Dad's worn address book in search of his accountant's number.

With the phone pressed to my ear, I pray Carroway will tell me what I want to hear—that Dad has funds tucked away, that money isn't a problem. To make bail, we'll need to come up with a hundred grand for the bondsman.

Carroway answers in the same measured tone I remember from childhood, when he'd show up in his pressed suits for meetings with Dad. "I thought I might hear from you. I heard what happened in court today. Unfortunately, I don't have great news."

My chest tightens. "Just tell me, Mr. Carroway. Can Dad cover the bond?"

Papers rustle in the background. "Your father's assets are substantial, but not liquid. Most of his wealth is in land. He has investments—stocks and bonds—managed by Preston Hartwell at Hartwell Capital Advisors. If Hartwell liquidates, he might be able to raise half the bond amount by close of business today. But that's a big maybe."

"We have to try. I'll call him right now. Do you have the contact information?"

"Yes, I'll send it over right away." A pause. "Lane, there's something else you should know. Your father recently granted you power of attorney."

I blink hard. "He . . . what?"

"Granted you power of attorney. I suspect he knew his memory was failing and wanted to make sure someone he trusted could handle his affairs."

I swallow hard past the lump in my throat. "When did he do this?"

"The documents came through my office a few months ago."

I sink into a chair, stunned. So Dad knows. He *knows* he's losing his mind. The thought shatters me more than the bail amount ever could. "And Judd?"

"As far as I know, your brother was not included in that arrangement. But you should confirm with Evan McCray. He drafted the documents."

"Okay. In the meantime, can you send me a summary of the accounts you have access to? I need to know what I'm dealing with. Not just for the bail, but for his future."

"I'm on it," Carroway says. "I'll send those over within the hour. And I'm forwarding you Preston Hartwell's contact information now."

My phone pings before we even hang up.

I immediately dial Hartwell. He answers on the first ring, already aware of the charges and the million-dollar bail. "I can start liquidating as soon as you give me the authorization."

"Do it," I say. "Whatever you can move today."

He repeats what Carroway told me—we'll be lucky to get fifty thousand by close of business.

When I end the call, my hands are shaking. Fifty thousand short. I stare out at the creek, trying to figure out where I'm going to find that kind of money.

Lally steps onto the porch, a dish towel in her hands. "Hey, sweet girl. I didn't want to bother you while you were on the phone. How're you holding up?"

"We're in trouble, Lally. The judge—"

"I heard. I was in the courtroom." She shakes her head. "The town's outraged. At least the good folks who know your father—the ones he gave second chances to. Men he sent to rehab instead of prison. Folks he helped find work when nobody else would take them. They remember, and they'll stand by him." She rests a hand on my shoulder. "We're all here for you, Lane. Whatever you need."

"That means so much, Lally. Thank you."

"It's the least I can do." She pulls me to my feet and into her arms—the same arms that held me through my worst days after the accident. Her magnolia-scented perfume pulls me back to summers of my youth, to memories of Tommy I thought I'd buried long ago. It's been happening a lot lately—these small triggers that stir up the past. Maybe that's why I stayed away so long. Deep down, I knew that coming home would mean facing it—those unanswered questions that still haunt me. And now, with a detective's eye instead of a sister's, I'm not sure I want the answers I might find.

I pull back and manage a small smile. "I'm glad you're here."

"I'm always here for you, baby. You have so much on your plate right now. I asked my niece to stop by, but I understand if this isn't the right time."

"Let's wait. I'm not even sure we can afford to hire her. And if I don't get Dad out of jail, there won't be anyone for her to care for anyway."

"We'll get him out of jail, don't you worry." She cups my cheek, then lets her hand fall.

I glance up at my old bedroom window. "I should move back in here. At least I can be with Dad in the evenings and overnight."

"I can shift my hours," Lally says. "Instead of eight to four, I'll work nine to five. That'll give you a little more time to yourself during the day."

"That'd be great, Lally. Hopefully, it'll only be temporary." I inhale a shaky breath. "I'll go grab my things from the cottage. I need something to keep me busy while I'm waiting to hear from Mr. Hartwell."

"Your room's ready for you. I'll make you some lunch while you're gone," she says, disappearing inside.

Scout trots after me as I head to the guest cottage for my things. She sticks closer these days, her eyes following me everywhere. Does she understand Addie is gone? Or is she still waiting for her to come home?

Back in the main house, I push open the door to my old bedroom. I've never been a frilly girl, and the room shows it. The walls are painted a soft sky blue, the quilt on the bed stitched in shades of the river—deep navy, slate, pale aqua. Beneath my feet, a rag rug in the same cool hues hides the worn spots in the old heart pine floors. No curtains soften the window, just plain wooden blinds that let in the morning light. Matching white-painted end tables flank the brass bed, sturdy and unpretentious, like everything else in this room.

I unpack my clothes in the antique oak dresser and set Scout's bed near the door. She ignores it, of course, leaping onto mine. Curling into a tight ball, she fixes me with a look that dares me to make her move.

I laugh. "All right. We'll try it—as long as you don't snore, hog the bed, or kick me in your sleep."

I stretch out next to her, stroking the warm fur along her back. A fragile kind of peace settles over me in this room—the only place I've ever truly felt happy, back when I was a little girl with two older brothers and parents who still loved each other. I let my eyes drift shut, halfway to sleep, until Lally's voice floats up the stairs, calling me to lunch.

Swinging my legs over the side of the bed, I redo my ponytail, tuck my laptop under my arm, and drag myself down to the kitchen. A sandwich waits on the counter—white bread, Duke's mayo, the last of the summer tomatoes. I'm lifting one half when Mr. Hartwell calls.

I set the sandwich back down and snatch up my phone. "I hope you have good news."

"Nothing earth-shattering. As suspected, I can only raise fifty thousand for the bail. If you give me your banking information, I'll wire the funds shortly."

I slide my laptop closer, pull up my account, and give him what he needs. "Thank you, Mr. Hartwell."

I've only just hung up when Carroway calls. "I've emailed you the documents you requested. You can see for yourself—there's money in his 401(k), but it's tied up. We'd have to liquidate stocks, pay penalties and taxes, and even then, it would take weeks. As for his hard assets, I don't recommend selling unless you want to make the judge hopping mad. And again, that would take time you don't have."

I press my palm against the cool tile countertop, fighting the sinking feeling in my gut. "No, I don't want to make Dad mad. It's his money, after all. I'll figure something out."

"You're in a tight spot, Lane. I wish I could be of more help."

Clicking open his email, I scroll down the list of Dad's assets. Just like he said—land-rich, cash-poor. In hindsight, we've never lived lavishly. No luxurious trips. No fancy cars or designer clothes. Just comfortable. Steady. Content with the beauty of the farm around us.

At the bottom of the list, something stops me cold. Steady monthly withdrawals—five thousand dollars each. My pulse quickens as I click the entry, but the recipient's name has been redacted. To whom? And for what?

I shove the laptop away. I can't think about this right now. Sliding off the stool, I start pacing, chewing my fingernails to the quick.

The mudroom door creaks open. Heavy footsteps cross the tile, and Judd appears in the doorway.

I level my gaze on him. "Where have you been? You missed the arraignment."

"I had to work." He brushes past me and grabs a bottle of water from the refrigerator.

"If you have to work, why are you here now?"

"It's my lunch break." He spots the sandwich. "You gonna eat that?"

Before I can answer, he stuffs half of it in his mouth. I snatch the other half before he takes it too.

"I heard about the ridiculous bail," he says between bites. "Tate's a scumbag. I've seen him down at the marina, coming and going from his boat with his girlfriend. His wife deserves better than that."

Tate's wife was our second-grade teacher—homely but kind. "Who's his mistress?"

"Some tacky hottie. Runs a tattoo joint, if you can believe that." He opens the pantry, frowning at the near-empty shelves.

"I'm not surprised, honestly. What kind of boat does he own?"

"A thirty-five-foot Bertram." He digs through the fruit bowl for a banana. "What's with all the questions?"

"I'm a detective. It's my job." I meet his eyes, my tone flat. "Just filing information away for later."

He peels the banana, smirking. "So what're you gonna do about the bail?"

My mouth drops open. "What am *I* gonna do?"

He shrugs. "You're the detective. You're in charge."

I return to my vacated barstool. "I can throw in thirty grand."

His eyes widen. "You've got thirty thousand dollars just lying around?"

"It's my divorce settlement. I never wanted it, but my attorney insisted. It's been sitting untouched, and I can't think of a better use than getting Dad out of jail. What about you? Can you contribute anything?"

A flush creeps up his neck. "I've saved a little for the baby. But Brandy would kill me if I touched it."

I roll my eyes. "Of course. Never mind your father's rotting in jail for a crime he didn't commit."

His jaw hardens. "Are you sure about that? Folks say there's another eyewitness."

I stare at him, stunned. "So they say. But I'm not buying it. I'll prove Dad's innocence—as soon as I get him out."

Lally bustles into the room, and Judd lets out a hoot, hooking an arm around her and swinging her in circles.

She laughs, swatting at him. "Stop, you naughty boy! I'm too old for your shenanigans."

He sets her down gently. She smooths her dress, cheeks flushed. "What're you doing here anyway? Can I fix you a sandwich?"

"I'd love that, but make it to go. I need to get back to work."

I backhand him in the gut. "Can't you say please?"

He presses his hands together under his chin. "Please, Lally. Pretty please."

She musses his hair. "Of course, sweet boy. Anything for you."

After he leaves, I take my laptop out to the porch and spend an hour on the phone with a loan officer. If I apply for a line of credit, the paperwork and approval process could take days. And Dad's already spent two nights too many in jail.

Around three o'clock, Lally calls me to the front door. "Come quick, Lane! You've gotta see this."

She swings the front door wide, and we step onto the porch.

A line of Tidewell locals stretches down the walk—some I know, some I don't. Mason jars and envelopes clutched in their hands. Folded checks. Faces filled with resolve.

Earl Givens, the hardware store owner, steps forward. "Afternoon, Lane. Word is you're struggling to raise the judge's bail. What Tate did, setting it so high, is a disgrace. We pooled what we could. Even the Methodist ladies passed the plate. Altogether, it's twenty thousand."

He hesitates, holding out the envelope. "I know it's not enough—"

"It's exactly what I need," I say, my voice trembling. "And I'm so grateful. But I can't accept it."

His face falls. "Why not? Every single one of us has a Judge Sutherlin story. He's given second chances, lent a hand when no one else would. Hollis is one of the finest men Tidewell's ever known. What's happening to him—the disease, these bogus charges—it's unfair."

Tears blur my vision as murmurs of agreement ripple through the crowd.

Someone calls out, "Your daddy didn't kill nobody. Hollis won't even hunt—says he can't stand to shoot a bird. Even them geese that mess all over his dock."

I laugh through the tears, swiping them away. "So true."

I study their faces—every color, every age. These humble people are the backbone of Tidewell. They carried us through Tommy's death, and they're here again now. Honest, hardworking, decent people. They deserve better than Vernon Tate.

An idea sparks in my mind. It's a long shot, but worth a try.

I meet Givens's eyes, then sweep the crowd. "I've spent the afternoon trying to come up with a solution. I have one more trick up my sleeve. If it doesn't work, I'll accept your generosity, but only with the promise that every cent will be paid back."

Roars of protest rise, and I hold up my hand to quiet them. "No argument. Either way, I'll make sure Dad knows you stood up for him today. He'll be as touched as I am."

As the crowd slowly drifts back down the walk—mason jars and envelopes tucked under arms—I stand on the porch with tears drying on my cheeks. Scout leans into my leg, her steady warmth anchoring me.

Vernon Tate can hide behind his bench. Clay Dalton can play his games. But they have no idea who they're up against. These people—these ordinary, extraordinary citizens—are behind us, and that means the world. With their faith to steady me, I'll get Dad out. And I'll prove the truth or die trying.

Time to pay the prosecutor a visit.

Chapter Fifteen

Briggs is leaning back in his chair, boots propped on his metal desk, munching on a Snickers bar when I walk in. He jerks upright so fast he nearly topples over, sending the trash can skittering across the tile. When he bends over to set it right, he smacks his head on the edge of the desk.

I cross my arms, smirking. "Don't let me interrupt."

He straightens, rubbing his temple, trying to salvage what's left of his dignity. "Well, well . . . Lane Sutherlin. I thought that was you today in the courtroom." Coming around the desk, he gives me a slow once-over, the old Lawson charm flashing in his baby-blue eyes. "You're not the little girl I remember. You're a full-blown woman."

"We all grow up eventually. Well, most of us." I let my gaze slide over him—sandy hair, baby blue eyes, those same damn dimples. "You haven't changed much either. I figured you'd be a politician by now. You were always such a suck-up."

He chuckles. "Nah. Too honest for politics. I heard you got married."

I nod. "And divorced. You?"

"Same."

I'm not surprised he got married—he's a catch. But I am

surprised someone let him go. "Have you been living in Tidewell all this time?"

"I went to New York with my wife, my college sweetheart. She made it big as a fashion designer. Turns out big-city living isn't for me. We both changed. Fell out of love." He spreads his arms with a grin. "So here I am, right back where I started. Living the dream." He gestures toward a chair—an uncomfortable, straight-back wooden thing that reminds me of high school detention. "I assume this isn't a social call."

I lower myself into the chair, the wood biting into my spine, and remind myself why I came. This isn't about catching up, or old crushes, or trading barbs.

"I'm here about my father. Obviously. His attorney will file a formal request to have the bail lowered, but it'll take too long, and Tate will likely deny it. Dad has no business in jail."

Briggs leans back, his chair squeaking. "I'm not so sure about that. Not after meeting with him yesterday afternoon. The Judge Sutherlin I remember was a kind, gracious man—sharp mind, fine palate, a lover of jazz. But the man I spoke with yesterday was dazed and confused . . . unsure of where he even was." He pauses, letting it hang before adding quietly, "In that state of mind, Lane, anything's possible."

Irritation prickles my skin. "Dazed and confused means he gets lost or forgets to take his meds. It doesn't mean he murders his daughter's best friend in cold blood."

He taps his pen on the desk, each click ratcheting my nerves tighter. "Some forms of Alzheimer's can twist a person into someone else entirely. A kind man becomes paranoid—sometimes even violent enough to kill."

"That's a little extreme, don't you think?" I shoot back, though part of me knows he's right.

"Not at all. When we go to trial, experts will testify to it."

Anger spikes through me. *Trial? Will it really go that far?*

I lean forward, my voice sharp. "So you're going after Hollis?

You, of all people? He was like a father to you after you lost your own."

Briggs flinches. "That's not fair. I'm doing my job. *My* bail request was justified. I had no idea Tate would double it."

"Yeah, but you didn't argue, which makes you guilty by association. I'm barely scraping together ten percent for the bondsman. Dad's condition will nosedive in jail."

"Arguing is pointless with a man like Tate," Brigg deadpans.

I roll my eyes. "And you call yourself a prosecutor." I tap my fingernail against his desk. "Get Tate on the phone. Demand he lower it. With Dad's reputation, he should've been released on his own recognizance. There's no case here, Briggs. These charges are trumped up. So he was fishing near the boathouse—big deal. He had no idea she was there."

"There's a witness, Lane. This is serious."

I stare him down. "Have you questioned this witness? Is he credible?"

"He knows your father. He swore it was him."

"You're ignoring my question, Briggs. Is the witness credible?"

Briggs won't meet my eyes. "You're forgetting something important. Hollis has no alibi."

"Boone spoke to him around midnight when they were searching the area. Dad was in his pajamas. He'd been asleep. Maybe he doesn't remember earlier in the evening. That's dementia, Briggs, not guilt. He probably made dinner, watched TV, and went to bed. Nothing unusual. Nothing to remember."

Something shifts in Briggs's expression—his features softening just enough to tell me I'm getting through. I press harder. "If he had cancer and was undergoing chemo, would you keep him in jail?"

He exhales slowly. "That's different. But . . ." He steeples his fingers beneath his chin, eyes narrowing in thought. "I see your point."

I nod at his desk phone. "So you'll call him?"

With a heavy sigh, Briggs reaches for the receiver. "I'll try."

When I hear the line ringing, I lean over the desk, close enough not to miss a word.

"Tate here," the judge answers gruffly.

Briggs lowers his voice, slipping into the same schmoozing tone I remember all too well. "Afternoon, Judge. Lawson Briggs here. I need to talk to you about the Sutherlin case. Considering his health, I'm requesting he be released immediately on his own recognizance."

The judge barks out a laugh. "Never!"

"Then cut it to five hundred thousand—my original recommendation." Briggs repeats my chemo argument word for word, his voice steady and persuasive.

"Sorry, son. But this case is too important. I'm under pressure. My hands are tied."

Before I can think better of it, I snatch the receiver from Briggs. "Hello, Vernon. Lane Sutherlin here. Tell me—who's tying your hands? Your little mistress, the tattoo artist?"

Briggs goes pale, then fights a smile—half horrified, half impressed. He makes a grab for the receiver, too late.

"You have some nerve, Sutherlin," Tate says, voice low and dangerous.

"I don't care about your sordid little affair," I reply. "But your wife might be interested in how you spend your afternoons on that thirty-five-foot Bertram. She was my second-grade teacher, you know."

"Are you threatening me, young lady?" His tone is ice cold. In one breath, I understand I've just made an enemy of Vernon Tate —not my smartest move.

"No, sir. Just pointing out how loose lips get after a couple of whiskeys at Slip 99. If you catch my drift." My tone is calm. My heart hammers.

The line goes quiet, long enough for me to picture my own untimely death on a lonely highway.

"Release on recognizance is out of the question," Tate says at last. "But . . . I will honor Briggs's original recommendation. Half a million. Not a penny less. And if word of this conversation gets out, Ms. Sutherlin, I will see you cited for contempt of court."

The line goes dead, and I drop the receiver into its cradle. "Watch and learn, Briggs."

"That was reckless, Lane. Tate doesn't forget insults. He'll come after you now."

"No, he won't. You and I both know about his affair. If I suddenly disappear, you'll know what happened to me. That would be reckless of him."

Briggs stares at me like I've grown two heads. "Do you hear what you just said? Thanks to you, I now know about the affair. That makes me just as much of a target."

Guilt surges, sharp and sudden. He's right. In my determination to get Dad out of jail, I've put Briggs's life in danger. "I'm so sorry. I—"

He waves me off, a grin tugging at his mouth. "Relax. Tate's as corrupt as the day is long. I'd love nothing more than an excuse to go after him. You just might've handed me one." The grin fades, replaced by something sharper. "But you, Lane—you're the wild card. He'll be watching you now."

"I'm a big girl, Briggs. I can take care of myself."

"I can see that." His smile tugs wider, a glint of admiration flickering. He pushes to his feet. "Now, go see the bondsman. And take collateral. He's a good guy—he'll work with you."

I leave Briggs's office with my pulse still hammering. Part of me wants to grin—I went toe to toe with Vernon Tate and walked out with a small victory. But another part of me knows I just painted a target on my back. *That was reckless, Lane.* Reckless as hell. The same kind of behavior that got me suspended in Richmond. Morales says I'm walking a tightrope because of my divorce. But maybe this is just who I am. Or maybe it's the unfinished business from my past, clawing its way back to the surface.

Chapter Sixteen

Briggs was right. The bondsman is a good man. He lets me use Dad's boat for collateral. The old tub of rust isn't worth a dollar, let alone fifty thousand. But Derek Barlow, like most folks in this town, knows Dad isn't a flight risk.

Afterward, while I'm waiting for Dad to be discharged, I stop by Boone's office. He's slouched behind his desk, arms folded, massaging his jaw, his expression a million miles away. He startles when I appear in the doorway.

"Lane!" He waves me in. "I was just thinking about you—wondering how you managed to get Vernon Tate, meanest son of a bitch this side of the Mississippi, to cut your daddy's bail?"

I chuckle and drop into the chair across from him. "If I told you, I'd have to kill you."

His brow pinches. "Don't joke about that. If we're going to work together, we need to trust each other. No secrets."

"I get it, Sheriff. But this one's better left unsaid. Safer for you that way."

He narrows his eyes. "You've got something on him."

"Maybe." I let a sneaky smile slip.

Come to think of it, Judd works at a busy marina. If he knows about Tate's fling with the tattoo gal, others probably do too.

Boone studies me a long moment, suspicion flickering across his face. "I'll let it slide this time. But watch yourself, Laney. Your daddy will never forgive me if anything happens to you."

"I'll be careful, I promise."

"So the bail's squared away?"

"Yes, sir. Dad's being discharged as we speak."

"I heard the town tried pooling money. You did right, turning them down. Tidewell folks will give you the shirts off their backs."

"True. I appreciate their generosity, but I couldn't take their hard-earned cash." I lean forward, elbows on my knees. "Now we need to get these charges dropped and clear Dad's name. Have you learned anything else about the mysterious eyewitness?"

He shakes his head. "Not yet. Nobody's talking."

"Apparently, the man knows Dad, but Briggs won't vouch for his credibility. Something's fishy."

Boone grunts. "Agreed. We'll keep digging." He pushes back from his chair and hauls himself up. "Come on. Let's go check on Hollis. I bet he's ready to get home."

"I just hope I can keep him there," I mutter.

I find Dad downstairs, holding court like a movie star on the red carpet—shaking hands, trading laughs, saying goodbye to every friend he's made in lockup. But he says little on the drive out to the farm. He stares out the window, his eyes glassy, lips pressed in a firm line—a million miles away. If only I knew what was going through his mind.

As we pass under the canopy of river birch trees, I glance over at him. "Lally picked up steaks for dinner. But we can order takeout if you'd rather. It's up to you."

He turns from the window, a soft smile tugging at his lips. "Steak sounds good. I'd like to shower first, then I'll marinate them."

I offer to carry his bag, but he insists on taking it upstairs himself. "I'm not an invalid, Bug. At least not yet."

Still, I trail him up the stairs, pretending I need to change.

Truth is, I'm afraid to let him out of my sight. We can't risk him wandering off again. Or worse, getting lost. If word got out, Briggs could use it against him in court.

When I hear the shower running, I head back downstairs, locking the front door on my way to the kitchen.

Scout's crunching kibble when Dad reappears, freshly shaven, hair still damp.

"You need a haircut, Dad."

He rakes his fingers through the long locks curling behind his ear. "I'm going for the Ernest Hemingway look," he teases. And just like that, my dad is back.

I laugh. "Now that you mention it, you have that Hemingway vibe working. Next thing I know, you'll be growing a mustache and beard."

"Don't count on it. I've never been much on facial hair."

He fiddles with the music app on his phone, and Van Morrison's sultry voice fills the kitchen.

"What? No Louis Armstrong tonight?"

"Not tonight. Laney's choice. My way of thanking you for getting me out of jail."

I slip an arm around his waist. "You'd have done the same for me."

"I'm a retired judge. You never would've been arrested in the first place." He winks at me, and for a moment, it's as if nothing has changed—like time rolled back twenty years.

After Judd left for college, Dad and I had two years here alone, just the two of us. Every night was like this—cooking dinner, music in the background, talking through our day. He'd tell me about his cases—probably more than he should have. I was never cut out for law school, but turns out, detectives and judges aren't so different. We both dig for truth—just in different dirt.

A few minutes later, we're outside by the grill—Dad tending the steaks—when he says quietly, "If only I could remember where I was Thursday night."

I nod. "That would be great. Maybe if we retrace your steps, you'll remember something—anything—that might help us figure it out."

"We can try," Dad says, though his tone carries no hope.

"Let's move backward through time. What were you doing when Boone stopped by around midnight, searching for Addie?"

"Sleeping, of course."

"Do you still go to bed around ten? Read a little before turning out the light?"

He grins. "Every single night of my life."

"What time do you usually eat dinner?"

"Seven o'clock. I've gotten in the habit of watching the news while I eat." He opens the grill and flips the steaks.

"Do you remember what you ate that night?"

"I ordered a pizza." The answer comes quick, without hesitation. "There was no food in the house. I should've let Lally go to the store when she offered."

This is good. I remember Lally saying she offered to go to the store, and I can easily confirm the pizza delivery.

"So you ate pizza, watched the news, then went to bed?"

He frowns, shaking his head. "Except . . . there's something missing. I went somewhere after dinner. My memory is fuzzy, Bug, like I drove the car into a dense fog. I'm not sure where."

Goosebumps crawl across my skin. "Did you meet someone for drinks?"

He considers. "I don't think so. It wasn't like that. I had a meeting . . . but I don't think it was planned."

The bottom drops out of my stomach. I feel sick. Briggs's words echo in my mind. *Some forms of Alzheimer's can twist a person into someone else entirely. A kind man becomes paranoid—sometimes even violent enough to kill.*

Does that mean a man can seem perfectly normal one minute, then unrecognizable the next?

Noticing his frustration, I rest a hand on Dad's shoulder. "Don't worry about it anymore tonight. This is helpful. We can ask around tomorrow. Maybe we'll connect the dots."

Problem is, Judd and I have already spoken to all his friends about that night. None of them saw him. If he wasn't meeting a friend, then who? And why?

"What dots?" he asks, jabbing the steaks with his fork, piling them onto a plate.

"The dots to help us remember where you were on Thursday night," I explain.

He nods, lifting the plate of steaks. "Oh, right."

I fear the dementia has taken over again, but once we sit down at the table, he seems alert.

"Have they set a date for Addie's funeral?" he asks. "I'd like to go, but all things considered, I'm not sure I'd be welcome."

"No funeral plans yet. The medical examiner hasn't completed the autopsy."

As he pours wine into our glasses, my gaze shifts to the security panel on the wall behind him, just outside the mudroom door. The green light glows solid—ready to alarm—even though we haven't used it in years. My parents had it installed, not to keep intruders out but to keep my brothers in during their wild teenage years.

"So, Dad. Do you remember the alarm code? I feel a little unsettled with everything going on. Maybe if I set it tonight, we'll both sleep better."

He looks up from his plate, expression grim. He knows exactly what I'm thinking—the alarm will sound if he tries to leave during the night. "Sure, Bug. It's five-five-five-five. Same code I use for everything else."

After dinner, Dad digs two bowls of ice cream from the freezer, just like old times. Scout sprawls at our feet while Van Morrison croons through the speakers. We even turn on the gas logs, though the night is still warm, the flicker of flames making the family room glow soft and golden. For a little while, it almost feels normal—like the three of us can pretend life hasn't splintered apart.

But his words at the grill won't leave me. *I had a meeting.* They circle my brain long after I tuck him into bed and set the alarm. I lie awake, listening for the rise and fall of his breath down the hall, wishing for rest, knowing it won't come. If he really did go out that night . . . who did he meet? And why?

By morning, my head is heavy from too little sleep. The scent of coffee pulls me downstairs, Scout trotting ahead. Dad is already at the kitchen table—showered, shaved, tortoise glasses perched on his nose—the picture of calm authority. For a split second, he looks every inch the judge again—the father I remember.

He glances up as if he's been waiting for me.

"Good morning, Laney Bug." His voice is chipper, like he's about to tell me Virginia finally beat Virginia Tech in football. "I remember where I was Thursday night."

The mug nearly slips from my hand. "Where?"

He folds his glasses and sets them aside. "I went to see Roxie."

Chapter Seventeen

I shake my head, not sure I heard him correctly. "Did you just say you went to see Roxie?"

"Yes." His smile disappears. "Trouble is, I can't for the life of me remember why?"

I collapse into the nearest chair. "She probably wanted to borrow money."

"Why? Her husband has plenty. Anyway, I'm fairly certain I initiated the meeting. I may even have shown up unannounced." His eyes go cloudy, face soft with memory. "I still miss her sometimes, you know. We were together for twenty-five years. She gave me three amazing kids."

"Maybe you went there to remind her of that. She seems to have forgotten about us." My pulse spikes. "Wait—if this is true, if you really were with her Thursday night, why hasn't she offered you an alibi?"

His brow furrows. "That's the part I'm not sure about. Maybe she hasn't heard about my arrest."

"Trust me, she's heard. Everyone in Tidewell knows. Everyone in *Virginia* knows." Heat flares in my chest. "We can sit here and speculate all morning, or we can get answers." I'm already on my feet, taking the stairs two at a time.

Fifteen minutes later—showered, dressed, and fueled by righteous fury—I'm ready to catch a thief. Or at least read my mother the riot act.

First, though, I need to feed the dog. Scout is sprawled on the sofa, sleeping so soundly I have to nudge her off just to get her to eat. She's taken to her new accommodations, even claimed the leather chair in Dad's study last night. After all she's been through, she deserves the day off.

I greet Lally at the door when she arrives at nine, kissing her cheek on my way out. "I'm off on a lead. Keep an eye on him today. I'm leaving Scout here to keep him company. Call me if you need me."

I drive across the river, pushing the speed limit, to Oyster Bay Estates—a gated community in the new section of town. All the houses are cookie-cutter mansions with treeless yards and enough square footage to make sure you never have to actually see your family. Perfect little McEstates with identical stone façades and three-car garages lined up like soldiers. The kind of place where landscapers roll through once a week so the homeowners can pretend they have green thumbs.

Roxie gave me a sticker for my car window years ago. I'm not sure why. She never invited me to her house. Maybe it was just easier than pretending she would.

When I roll down my window at the guardhouse, the security officer—a young man, no more than twenty, drowning in a polo two sizes too big—frowns at me. "You've got your sticker. You don't need to sign in."

I lean out the window. "Actually, I need you to check your log for Thursday night? Look for Hollis Sutherlin."

"You the po-po or something?"

I flash my badge. "Something."

The kid flips a few pages, running his finger down the column. "Here it is. Signed in around eight o'clock, left after nine. Did he rob somebody's house?"

I snort. "No. He's a retired judge—spent thirty years putting people in jail for that exact thing. Ask your grandpa. I'm sure he's heard of him."

I peel away, then slam on the brakes and throw it in reverse, rolling back to the guardhouse. "One more thing. What's the McDaniels' address?"

His brow knits. I can see the question forming in his mind—why would I have a resident sticker if I don't even know the address? After a beat, he checks his roster. "410 Bayview Drive. Should I ring Mrs. McDaniel to let her know you're coming?"

A smirk tugs at my lips. "No. I'm her daughter. I'd rather it be a surprise."

Truth be told, I don't need Roxie's address. Even though I've only been here twice, I can easily spot the monstrosity—a bad imitation of a Tuscan villa—half Olive Garden, half Caesars Palace. Terracotta roof tiles, arched doorways, and enough columns to make the Parthenon jealous. Roxie's house doesn't just sit on the street—it struts. Front and center on the biggest lot in the neighborhood, showing off that terracotta roofline like a crown while the other houses bow in line behind it. And, of course, she snagged the prime view of Oyster Bay. If Tidewell ever held a parade of gaudy McMansions, Roxie's place would be the grand marshal.

Money can buy a lot of things, but apparently, taste isn't one of them.

In a driveway large enough to land a small plane sits a gleaming white Jaguar convertible, an upgrade from her old Mercedes sedan. Of course, Roxie would trade up. Flashier, louder, more conspicuous—that's her brand.

When I bang the heavy iron knocker, none of her gray-uniformed staff comes to the door. Small mercies—I'm spared the interior—a sea of marble surfaces and blinding white paint.

Circling the stone path to the waterside of the house, I find Roxie seated at a table by the pool—auburn hair coiled high on her head, yellow-striped umbrella shielding her creamy complexion from the morning sun. She's tapping her phone with a manicured nail, one long leg extended through the slit of her black satin robe.

The pool deck is marble—of course it's marble—so blinding it looks like someone's paid to polish it hourly. A gardener crouches nearby, trimming the grass along the edge of the pool deck with a pair of scissors, pausing just long enough to sneak glances at her legs.

When my boots hit the marble, Roxie looks up from her phone, finger frozen in midair. "Laney Bug! What a wonderful surprise!"

"Don't lie. And don't call me that."

She sets her phone on the table. "Oh, right. Only Daddy Dearest is allowed."

"Exactly. You lost that privilege when you walked out on us."

I turn away, and for a moment, the view steals my words. Oyster Bay stretches out below—McDaniel royalty gazing down on the town peasants. The sun glitters off the water, sailboat masts sway in the marina, striped awnings and broad porches crowd the waterfront. A picture-perfect Tidewell postcard.

Our view at River Birch Farm is nothing like this—wooded lots across the creek, river birch trees leaning low over the water, their pale bark catching the light. Quieter. Older. More honest. Roxie was never comfortable in that world—the one that hints at old money but never has to speak of it. The truly wealthy know better than to talk about money at all.

I sit in the chair farthest from her. "Let's cut to the chase. I'm here about Dad's visit on Thursday night."

"What visit? I haven't seen your father in months." She doesn't bat a fake eyelash. Not a muscle in her face quivers. Either she's an expert liar, or Botox has frozen her expression. Probably both.

"Don't play dumb, Mother. His name's on the guest log. I already confirmed it with your guard at the gate."

"Now that you mention it, I vaguely remember him stopping by." She snatches up her phone, tapping on her calendar. "Was that Thursday? My, how time flies."

I glare at her. "Why didn't you tell anyone? You could've given him an alibi instead of letting him spend two nights in jail."

She drops the phone on the table with a clatter. "Alibi? Jail? I have no idea what you're talking about."

"Give me a break, Roxie. The whole town knows about his arrest."

"I rarely leave the plantation, darling." She sweeps an arm at her surroundings. "Why would I?"

Now she fancies herself Scarlett O'Hara. How is it possible I share her DNA? Maybe I was switched at birth.

"You mean Leigh Anne didn't tell you? I thought you two were tight."

Leigh Anne, the mayor's wife, parades as Mom's best friend. But everyone knows the only thing holding them together is money for her husband's reelection.

Roxie twirls a strand of hair. "She may have mentioned it."

"To refresh your memory, Dad's been accused of Addie's murder. He can't remember where he was that night. Turns out, he was with you. So now you can clear his name."

"I'd rather not get involved." She inspects the lock for split ends.

I throw my hands up. "Fine. We'll subpoena you, and if you perjure yourself under oath, you'll go to jail. And you better believe Boone won't give you the white-glove treatment he gave Dad."

Roxie neatly tucks the strand of hair back into her updo. "Why do you hate me so much, Lane?"

"How can you even ask me that?"

Her face hardens. "Get to the point, Lane. I need to get dressed. I have a busy day ahead. Since you already know every-thing, what do you want from me?"

"Why was Dad here? What did he want?"

She stares out across Oyster Bay, her expression softening just enough to suggest there might be a heart buried in there somewhere. "Looking for sympathy. He's worried about his mental decline."

"And what did you tell him?"

She shifts her gaze back to me, her gray eyes as cold as storm clouds gathering over the bay. "To see a doctor."

I was wrong. She's heartless. "Thanks for nothing." I spring to my feet and retrace my steps along the stone path.

"Wait, Lane!"

I turn. "What?"

"Keep this between us, will you? I don't want to upset Lawrence."

Lawrence? Who the hell is Lawrence? "You mean Larry?"

She lifts her chin. "He goes by Lawrence now. And I'm Roxanne."

I laugh, biting back the comment on my tongue. "You're the mother of his children. Why would *Larry* care if Dad wanted to talk to you about his health?"

"He was out of town. He doesn't like me having male guests while he's gone."

I tilt my head. "Do you have male visitors often?" My hand shoots up. "Never mind. Don't answer that. I don't want to know."

As I continue around to the driveway, I can't help but wonder if Larry is jealous of Dad. Hollis is a respected judge—loved across the community. Meanwhile, Larry spends his days in Las Vegas and the Bahamas, dabbling in God-knows-what shady business that bankrolls this circus.

Chapter Eighteen

My hands shake as I speed away from Roxie's faux Caesars Palace. Roxie gets under my skin worse than Judd—they're cut from the same cloth. Good thing I take after Dad.

I need comfort. Instead of donuts, I stop by the Salty Bean for a maple pecan latte. The scent of roasted beans and cinnamon syrup hits me before the bell over the door stops ringing.

I buy an extra and head down the block to Crown & Glory. When I open the door, I'm hit with a blast of Justin Timberlake—Trina's tribute to Addie. I can't believe we ever listened to this garbage, ever thought he was hot.

I wave at Trina, careful not to disturb her client, and grab a magazine. Sinking into a chair, I sneak glances over the top. In all the years I've known her, I can't remember once seeing her without makeup—not mornings before school, not late nights after parties. Never a smeared lash or crooked lip. Now, her eyes are swollen slits, her nose rubbed raw. Her pink T-shirt is inside out, tag sticking up, soggy tissues tucked beneath both sleeves.

She runs clippers over her client's head, buzzing him nearly bald. He looks at the hair on the floor, then back at Trina in the mirror. But he doesn't complain. He knows she's suffering.

She waits until he leaves before breaking. "This is just awful, Lane. I never considered the possibility that she might be . . . you know . . . dead." Her voice is meek, her face so utterly lost.

"I know," I say, taking her in my arms.

"I don't know what I'll do without her. I can't run this place alone. My receptionist has gone dark on me. She's convinced whoever did this to Addie will come after us too."

"Why don't you close the salon for a couple of days? Your clients will understand."

"No, they won't!" Trina pushes me away and staggers to her stylist chair. "People are counting on us—on me. I was slammed before. Now I have Addie's clients to take care of as well."

When she starts sobbing hysterically, I lock the door and flip the sign to *Closed*. I pull up a chair beside her, murmuring whatever soothing things come to mind. But when her breathing turns fast and shallow, panic rises in my throat. She's hyperventilating. Not good.

"Hey, hey—look at me." I grip her shoulders lightly. "You're okay, Trina. Just breathe with me, all right? In . . . two, three. Out . . . two, three."

Her eyes flutter open. I exaggerate the motion, pulling air through my nose, then blowing it out slowly through pursed lips. "Good. Just like that. You're doing great."

I breathe with her until her shoulders relax and the color returns to her face.

"You're not in this alone, Trina. You have friends who will help you. You'll hire another stylist, and this place will run smoothly again before you know it."

I fill a cup of water from the cooler and press it into her hand. "Here. Small sips."

A customer bangs on the glass. I crack the door open to an elderly woman. "I'm sorry, but we're closed for the rest of the day."

The woman bristles. "What? Why didn't Trina call to cancel?"

"She's preoccupied. She just lost her best friend and business partner. She needs a little empathy and patience right now."

The woman huffs. "Well, I *need* my hair colored. Tell her to call me as soon as she's back at work."

Trina gestures weakly toward the door. "See what I'm dealing with?"

"With clients like her . . ." I lean against the counter. "What the heck? You don't need clients like her." I make a goofy face at the door, and to my relief, Trina laughs. Then I do too—until we're both doubled over, laughing through the tears.

When the moment passes, Trina slumps back in her chair, letting out an audible sigh. "That felt good. I don't remember the last time I laughed like that."

"Go home and hug your kids. Take the rest of the week off— two weeks if you need it. Your clients can wait. They survived the pandemic, didn't they?"

Trina cuts her eyes at me. "Barely. I was cutting hair out of my garage. It's a wonder the health department didn't shut me down." She pushes to her feet and brushes herself off. "I'll be fine. I always am."

I spin her around to face the mirror. "Look at yourself. You're a mess. You nearly cue-balled your last client. Do that to the wrong man, and you'll be out of business for good."

Tears well, and she drops her gaze. "I guess you're right."

"When you're feeling better in a few days, put the word out that you're hiring. See if any stylists in town are looking to make a change."

She blows her nose loudly, tossing the tissue in the trash. "I've already got my eye on someone. She's green, but she has potential. She's currently working for Hank at the Barber Shop."

"See! You're already thinking ahead." I play-punch her arm.

"Sorry about the pity party." She places a hand on my face, thumbing my cheek. Her eyes glisten, red-rimmed but soft. "Look at you—strong as ever. You loved Addie too. And with your dad being accused of—" Her voice falters, catching on the word she can't say. "Well, it's the craziest thing I've ever heard. No one believes he's guilty."

Removing her hand from my face, she busies herself with combs and scissors. "I wasn't completely honest with you the other day. I didn't want to say anything, didn't want to betray Addie. She never confided in me, but I had this feeling something was off. Maybe if I'd said something sooner, she'd still be alive."

"Don't go there, Trina. You'll drive yourself crazy thinking like that." I pick up a brush and run it through her pixie cut. "How was she *off*? Tell me what you noticed."

She catches my wrist, stilling my hand. "It was just a hunch. She was buttoned up as always, but jumpy—skittish one minute, walking on air the next."

"Do you think she and Clay were having problems?"

She shakes her head fast. "Not Tidewell's golden couple. They were rock solid."

"Sometimes things aren't what they seem. Especially in a marriage. Take it from someone who knows firsthand."

"I'm sorry, Lane. I heard about your divorce."

I don't ask who told her. Judd told Brandy, and Brandy told two friends. Now, the rest of the town knows. "What do you think of Clay?"

Her eyes lift to mine in the mirror, uncertain but sharp. "You don't like him?"

"I didn't say that. Something about him doesn't sit well with me. I know for sure that I don't trust him."

Trina glances around, and even though the salon is empty, her voice drops to a whisper. "Don't let anyone in town hear you say that. Clay knows a lot of powerful people. You've been gone a long time, Laney. Things have changed around here."

She meets my gaze again in the mirror, eyes haunted. "There's a dark current rising with our tides. Everyone feels it, even if they won't admit it. Tidewell's not the same town you left."

A shiver runs down my spine. I can see it in her eyes—this

isn't just grief talking. Trina is afraid. And I have a sinking feeling I've brushed against something I'm not ready to face. Not yet.

Before I can answer, my phone buzzes against the counter. A text from Sheriff Boone.

Autopsy's finished. Meet me at the morgue.

Dread coils low in my gut. Whatever dark current Trina's talking about, I can feel it pulling at my feet.

Chapter Nineteen

The basement of Tidewell Regional feels more dungeon than hospital—damp walls, humming pipes, a chill that seeps straight into my bones. The elevator doors slide open, spilling me into a long corridor that smells faintly of bleach and death.

At the far end, outside the morgue, I spot Clay and Boone—heads close, voices low, too intent on each other to notice me. I slow my pace, catching fragments. Boone's defensive tone carries. "Her father was accused of the murder. She was digging anyway. I couldn't very well tell her no."

A smile tugs at my lips. *Busted.*

I close the distance. "Morning, gentlemen," I say brightly. "If you're talking about me, I'd like to hear the unabridged version."

Clay straightens, his mouth curving into that politician's smile he saves for cameras and funerals. "Funny you should pop up, Lane. I just got off the phone with Sergeant Morales in Richmond —he told me about your suspension." His gaze flicks over me, smug and knowing.

"Tidewell should feel honored to have your 'expertise.' " He hooks his fingers in air quotes. "Morales wouldn't part with the details. Care to share why he benched you?"

Morales would never have divulged information about me. But Milo would.

"We fight serious crime in Richmond, Clay—*big boy stuff*. Things get a little dicey sometimes. And for the record, it wasn't a suspension. I'd banked too much vacation time, so when Addie disappeared, Morales suggested I take a paid leave to clear my head." I give him a cool smile. "You know how stress can be."

So what if I'm stretching the truth? He doesn't need to know that.

I pivot toward Boone, keeping Clay in my peripheral. "Good news, Sheriff. We figured out Dad's whereabouts Thursday night."

Clay snorts, but the sound lands brittle. "You *figured* it out? Or you *fabricated* an alibi?"

I ignore him and train my gaze on Boone. "Dad finally remembered he went to visit Roxie. His name's in the guard log at Oyster Bay Estates."

Boone's expression softens—just for a moment—before he catches himself. He can't afford to show favoritism to an old friend. "Why on earth would Hollis visit Roxie?"

I shrug. "He says he still misses her sometimes, and he needed someone to talk to about his memory slipping."

Clay lets out a sharp huff, a smirk plastered on his face. "If that's true, why didn't Roxie speak up when he was arrested? Seems convenient to me."

"Apparently, Larry was out of town. She didn't want him knowing Hollis came by—guess he's jealous of her ex." I level my gaze on Clay. "Bottom line, she'll testify if necessary. So Dad's a dead end. You'll have to find someone else to pin your wife's murder on."

"Enough." Boone cuts in, voice firm, eyes flickering between us. "Knock it off. This isn't helping Addie."

The morgue door opens, and the medical examiner waves us inside. Dr. Naomi Chen is petite, even shorter than me, with shoulder-length dark hair and sharp brown eyes. She's pretty, in a polished, no-nonsense way—exactly the type you'd want poking around for the truth.

I've been in the Richmond morgue countless times, but seeing my best friend's body under a sheet—Addie, right there—rocks me to my core. I can't touch her. Can't see her smile. Just the stillness where she used to be.

"Thank you all for coming," Dr. Chen says. "The autopsy is complete, and the body will soon be released to her family for burial."

When she glances over at Clay, there's the faintest flicker in her brown eyes—something I can't quite read. Her shoulders stiffen, and she looks away too quickly. *Is she afraid of him?*

She hands Clay a plastic bag with Addie's personal effects: running clothes, pink sports bra, her Apple Watch. "Please check that everything is accounted for."

He barely looks inside before nodding. "Everything's there."

When he tries to hand it back, I snatch it away and check for myself before passing it to Chen. "What about her engagement and wedding rings?" I ask Clay. "Was she wearing them that night?"

Clay's face doesn't twitch, but his tone is flat, almost bored. *That kind of control takes effort.* "How would I know? We didn't keep those kinds of tabs on each other."

I press my hand to my pocket, where Addie's wedding band rests. "This is important. Maybe whoever killed her took them."

"Or maybe someone killed her *for* them." Clay's pale blue eyes flicker—the flash of relief at the possibility of another suspect. A way out. "Which supports my original theory that she was killed by a random drifter. I'll check at home, see if I can find the ring."

The ring. *Singular.* My pulse skips. Does he know the band was lost in the mud?

I nod slowly. "You do that."

Dr. Chen flips open her tablet and scans the report. "Estimated time of death was between nine and eleven on Thursday night. Cause of death: asphyxiation. She was strangled."

I'm not surprised. I saw the marks on her neck. "And the murder weapon? Not the killer's hands, I presume."

"No. An object." Dr. Chen taps the screen. "Not round like a rope, but about the same size, with pink nylon fibers."

"Like a dog's leash?" My eyes lock on Clay. He doesn't flinch. He's good. *Too* good. "She was out walking her dog when she disappeared, and I don't see the leash with her other effects."

Dr. Chen nods slowly. "Yes, most definitely could've been a leash."

I fight past the lump in my throat. "Addie had a matching set—pink leash with Scout's name and Addie's number stitched in white. I gave them to her as a gift when she got Scout. She's still wearing the collar."

My gaze shifts to Boone. "The leash wasn't found at the crime scene?"

He shakes his head. "Not that I'm aware. I'll double-check. We need to find that leash."

Dr. Chen lowers her tablet. "There's another matter—a highly sensitive one. The autopsy shows your wife was pregnant, about eight weeks along. I'm very sorry."

The room goes silent for a beat—the only sound the low hum of the fluorescent lights. Clay's face is unreadable—no gasp, no blink, nothing. Just that damn poker face.

Addie, pregnant? My throat tightens, pain cutting through my chest. The joy she never got to share.

I swallow hard, choosing my words carefully. "Dr. Chen, do you still have tissue samples preserved?"

"Yes, of course."

"Then I'd recommend we order DNA testing to confirm paternity." I can feel Clay's eyes burning into me, but I don't dare look his way. "We're working a murder investigation. We have to rule out every possible scenario."

Color creeps up Clay's neck, his composure cracking. "Absolutely not!"

Boone cuts in, his tone firm but calm. "I agree with Lane. We need the complete picture. If there's nothing to hide, the test will show it."

Chen rests a hand on Clay's arm. "If you'll consent, I can draw your blood before you leave. The state lab is fast-tracking this case —we should have results by Friday."

Clay huffs out a reluctant sigh. "Fine. I'll go along with it for the sake of the investigation." He grudgingly rolls up his sleeve. "Don't stick me too hard."

The sheriff settles his hat on his head. "All right. If that's all you've got, I'm gonna head out. Got some calls to return."

"I'll go with you," I say, grateful for the excuse to get Clay out of my line of sight and a chance to speak to Boone alone.

"After you." Boone motions me through the door.

I wait until the elevator doors close before broaching the subject. "With all due respect, Sheriff, Clay's a conflict of interest. He shouldn't be anywhere near Addie's case."

Boone fixes me with that tired, heavy look of his. "I'm aware, Lane. But I can't have folks thinking you're running this investigation. Clay stays. My call."

The doors open onto the main floor, and I follow him to the parking lot. "I understand, sir. But you have to see what he's doing here. Clay's steering this investigation wherever he damn well pleases."

We reach his cruiser, and Boone turns on me. "What're you saying, Lane? Are you suggesting Clay had something to do with his wife's murder?"

"I'm saying we have to consider every angle. You know the golden rule of homicide investigations—the spouse is the first suspect until proven innocent. And Clay?" My jaw tightens. "He's acting like a man desperate to shift blame. First Dad, because he happened to be fishing near the boathouse. And now a drifter, a thief, who supposedly killed Addie for her engagement ring."

Boone's brow furrows. "That sounds like a very real possibility to me."

I glare at him over the top of my sunglasses. "Seriously? In

Tidewell? When's the last time you arrested a vagrant for anything more than trespassing?"

He opens his mouth to speak, but nothing comes out.

"Next thing we know, Clay will be pointing a finger at the father of Addie's baby—whoever that turns out to be."

Boone removes his hat, scratching the back of his head, the lines around his eyes deepening. "You think sweet little Addie Dalton was having an affair?"

"Something was going on with her, Sheriff. In the message she left for me the night she was murdered, she said she'd gotten herself into trouble."

Boone exhales through his nose, arms folding across his chest. "Well now—you didn't tell me that."

"I told you she called. That she needed help." My pulse races. "If she was having an affair, you can bet Clay knew about it."

Boone's gaze hardens. "Watch your step, Sutherlin. You've been gone a long time. This isn't the sleepy little town you remember. Start throwing accusations about Clay killing his wife, and you'll have more enemies than friends before you can say jackrabbit."

"Yes, sir. Understood."

He studies me a moment longer. "Now, about your sudden leave of absence. I need to know the truth. What really happened?"

I clamp down on the surge of anger. "With all due respect, Sheriff, that's not your concern. What matters is finding who killed Addie."

His eyes narrow, but after a beat, he nods and slides behind the wheel. "Just be careful, Lane. This town doesn't bend easy. And it doesn't forget."

A chill snakes down my spine. That's the second time this morning I've been warned about Tidewell.

His cruiser rumbles to life and pulls away, leaving me alone in the lot. When I turn, I spot Clay lounging against the driver's side of my Bronco.

"Have a nice little chat with the sheriff?" he asks, smiling like the devil waiting his turn.

"Just getting some things straight."

He swings open my door with exaggerated politeness. "You really shouldn't leave it unlocked. Town's not as safe as it once was."

Oof. Make that three warnings.

I reach for the handle, but he steps into my path, close enough for his aftershave to claw at my senses—sharp, expensive, and sickening. "What do you want, Clay?"

He leans in close, his breath hot against my ear. "To warn you. I don't like you, Sutherlin. Never have. Tidewell doesn't need you stirring up trouble. Stay out of my way—or you'll regret it."

I hold his gaze. "Funny—you sound more worried about me stirring up trouble than about who killed your wife."

His steely eyes flicker—there and gone in an instant. Before I can press, he straightens, his face wiped clean, mask firmly in place. Just another grieving husband in the daylight. Then he saunters off with a loping gait, whistling under his breath like a man without a care in the world.

I slam my door, tires spitting gravel as I tear out of the lot. My hands are shaking as I stab at the call button on my dash.

Trina answers on the second ring, her voice thin and tired. "Lane? Everything okay?"

I pause a beat to catch my breath, reminding myself of her fragile state. "Just checking on you. Are you with your kiddos?"

"Not yet." I heard her fingers typing away on a keyboard. "But I'm taking your advice and closing the shop for the rest of the week. Once I finish canceling these appointments, I'm headed to see Mama Jean on my way home to my family."

"Give her a hug for me. I'll get by there soon." I slow my speed as I approach town. "You mentioned earlier that Addie seemed off—up one minute and edgy the next. Did she ever mention starting a family?"

"All the time! But she wasn't obsessing about getting pregnant. She just assumed it would happen when the time was right."

I think about her poor unborn child, never getting the chance to take its first breath. Was it even Clay's child? "Do you think she might have been seeing someone else?"

I expect Trina to jump to Addie's defense, but instead, a heavy silence fills the line. I picture her face—eyes wide, lips pressed tight. "Trina? Was Addie having an affair?"

Finally, she exhales a shaky breath. "Where'd you hear that?"

My heart hammers against my ribs. "I didn't *hear* it anywhere. I'm ruling out every possibility. Do you know something?"

"Not for sure. She was always leaving her phone lying around, though. A couple of times, I accidentally saw some texts. When I asked Addie about it, she said they were just friends."

My skin crawls with goosebumps. *Just friends.* That's what people always say before the truth blows their lives apart.

"Texts from who, Trina?"

The line goes quiet again—only her ragged breathing on the other end. Then, in barely a whisper, she says, "Ben Holloway."

Chapter Twenty

I drive aimlessly around town, my mind a million miles away —Roxie, Trina, Clay, Addie's unborn child. Around two, I snap out of my trance to find myself pulling into the City Marina lot.

I'm not here for food. It's well past lunchtime, and I haven't eaten all day, but the adrenaline coursing through me has killed my appetite. I just need to be somewhere that grounds me—somewhere warm and familiar where the world feels safe for five minutes. Slip 99.

Despite the late hour, the lunchtime rush is in full swing, laughter and the smell of fried shrimp rolling through the air. I spot an open stool at the far end of the bar and head that way.

Cooter greets me with a smile. "Hey, Lane. How you holding up? I'm sorry about Addie."

"Me too." Tears prick my eyes. The wound is still so fresh, every time someone offers condolences, I feel like they're pouring salt over it.

He slides a menu across the bar, and I push it back. "I'll have a half dozen oysters and a shot of tequila."

His head jerks back. "A bit early for tequila, isn't it?"

I arch a brow, fighting a smirk. "It's almost two. I figured your customers start drinking at breakfast."

He chuckles. "Bloody Marys. Not tequila. Other customers. Not you. I don't take you for a boozer."

I press my lips into a tight smile. "Some people pop pills or chew gummies. Tequila is my vice. But I never have more than one shot at a time."

"That's fair. Rough morning?"

I give a stiff nod. "You could say that."

"I'll get your order in. Shouldn't take long," he says, disappearing to the other end.

When he returns a minute later with the tequila, I ignore the lemon and salt and kick it back, savoring the burn as I slam the glass down on the bar.

"So, Cooter. I bet you hear a lot in here," I say, wiping my mouth with the back of my hand.

"More than I wanna know. You wouldn't believe some of the things customers say to one another, like I'm invisible. Couples talk dirty, women spill secrets, men brag about their sexual escapades—sometimes their wives, sometimes their mistresses." He grimaces. "Believe me, I wish I could tune them out." He holds his fingers to his ears, twisting like he's adjusting a radio dial. "Then there are the others, who treat me like their therapist. Problems, secrets—nothing's off the table."

"I bet." I trace a slow circle around the rim of the empty tequila shot glass. "So it's fair to say you know pretty much everything that goes on in this town."

"Pretty much." He slides me a wary look. "If you wanna ask me something, Lane, go ahead and ask."

"Put your finger on Tidewell's pulse—tell me what you feel."

"Ooh. I like these kinds of questions." He grins. "Easy one. Her pulse is strong. This old town's a fighter."

"Okay." I sit up taller, my back ramrod stiff. "Now you're her therapist. What's she telling you?"

His grin fades. Shoulders slumping, he shakes his head. "She's in a dark spot, Laney. Tidewell was built on faith, honor, integrity. Most folks are still honest, hardworking, God-fearing men and women. But outsiders are creeping in, threatening all that with their greed and corruption."

My heart sinks. So the warnings are true. "Do you think Tidewell will survive these outside forces?"

"I can't answer that. But I see the divide widening every day. I know on which side most folks fall. The evil's growing. The innocent is . . . not shrinking, exactly, but struggling to keep up."

"What do you think will happen?"

"Depends on which side stays in power." Someone down the bar hollers for a refill, and he grabs a mug, pulling a draft with practiced ease. "Addie's murder may be the spark that lights our civil war. You're Tidewell, born and raised. Maybe God brought you back for a reason."

"That's a tall order, Cooter."

"Maybe so. But if I were a betting man, I'd put my money on you." He delivers the beer, then returns with my oysters. "I'm sure old Hollis is glad to have you home. How's he doing? I heard he got released from jail."

"Yes! Thank heavens. Not only that, he remembered where he was the night Addie was killed. His alibi is solid. He's off the hook. Which reminds me, I need to call Lawson Briggs to get the charges dropped." I pick up my phone from the bar. "You don't have his cell number, do you?"

"I do. But save yourself a call. He just walked in the door."

Cooter waves Briggs over. "Just in time too. The guy sitting next to you was just leaving." He clears his throat pointedly.

The guy looks up. "I am?"

"Yep." Cooter nods at the clock above the bar. "Your boss'll send the posse after you if you don't get back to work."

The man follows his gaze to the clock, his eyes widening. "You ain't kidding. I didn't know it was so late." He jumps to his feet, fishing his wallet from his pocket.

Briggs waits while the man pays his check, then slides onto the stool beside me.

"Hey, Lane." His gaze flicks to the empty shot glass. "I could use a shooter. What're you having?"

"Tequila. One and done. You have a rough morning too?"

"Something like that. Feels like the earth tilted on its axis, and everything's out of whack."

I let out a dry scoff. "Join the club. That's today's theme."

Confusion crosses his face. "What'd I miss?"

I laugh, shaking my head. "Nothing." I slurp an oyster from its shell. "But I do have good news. I was just about to call you. You need to drop the charges against Dad." I fill him in on the discovery that Dad was with Roxie Thursday night—though she practically had to choke the words out.

"That is good news." He offers me a high five. "I'll take care of it right away."

Cooter stops by to take Briggs's order—a Caesar salad with fried oysters and a sweet tea. "Tate's gonna be madder than a red hornet."

"Why? He's a judge. Why would he want to keep an innocent man locked up?"

Cooter leans on the bar, lowering his voice. "Between you and me, he's always resented your father. The man stands for integrity—something Tate can't fake. And the way folks in this town love him? That burns him up."

"Dad's losing his mind. Isn't that enough for Tate?"

"Nothing's ever enough for Vernon Tate."

The volume in the restaurant suddenly dips—from a raucous mix of laughter and chatter to low murmurs and startled oohs.

I elbow Briggs. "Did you feel that? Something just shifted."

Briggs glances up at Cooter, who's scanning the crowd, brow furrowed. "What just happened?"

"Not sure. Something." Cooter grabs his phone from under the counter and scrolls through his texts. "My phone's blowing up. Apparently, the police are searching Ben Holloway's boat."

My heart lurches. "Ben's boat? Are you sure?"

Cooter nods, still thumbing through his phone. "Half the sheriff's department's down there. Folks are saying it looks bad."

I slide off my stool, tossing a few bills on the counter for the oysters I barely touched. "I was worried about this. Addie was last seen near there."

Briggs pulls out his phone. "I'll make some calls, see what I can find out."

"You do that." I grab my keys, then pause. "Give me your cell—I'll keep you posted too."

"That'd be great." He taps his screen. "Here. AirDrop."

A second later, my phone pings with his contact info. I hit accept, and his name pops up on my screen.

"Got it. Don't ignore my calls."

"Don't keep me hanging."

"Wouldn't dream of it." Without another word, I push through the crowd and head out the door, the noise of the bar fading behind me, muffled and distant, like a storm rolling in over the bay.

Chapter Twenty-One

B oone stands on the dock, arms folded tight across his chest, supervising the search when I arrive.

"What's going on?" I ask, sidling up beside him.

"Anonymous caller said Addie's belongings are on Ben's boat," he says without so much as a glance in my direction.

I arch a brow. "Another anonymous caller? That's an interesting pattern developing here, don't you think?"

"Don't know what to think, Sutherlin," he snaps, his voice gruff.

"You certainly didn't waste any time getting a search warrant," I say, unable to keep the accusation out of my voice.

He exhales through his nose. "That wasn't me. Clay pushed it through. Tate signed the warrant before I even knew what was happening."

"Sounds like somebody else is pulling your strings, Sheriff. Wonder who that might be?"

I bite back a sigh. Less than two hours ago, I warned him Clay was steering this investigation, and now, here we are.

Boone grunts. "If you're looking for an argument, you won't get one from me."

I brush past him and climb aboard. From the outside, it looks like every other houseboat tied up at Patriots Landing—a double-decker tin can with faded paint and rust bleeding down the sides. Inside is another story. Cypress paneling warms the walls of the narrow rooms. Stainless counters in the galley. A leather sofa. An oriental rug. Ben's boat isn't fancy, but it's cared for—minus the deputies yanking open drawers, putting his life into evidence bags.

Grabbing a pair of plastic gloves from the box, I stand off to the side, keeping out of their way. I watch them work with quiet efficiency, bagging lipstick tubes, a compact mirror, a sweater in the softest shade of pink—whispered intimacy, the everyday traces of two people tangled up in each other's lives.

Addie's been here. No doubt about that.

The discovery of a half-empty tampon box stops me cold. She was here during her last cycle—a month ago, maybe two. This wasn't a one-night fling. It was a long-term relationship.

The deputies glance at me sidelong as I hover in the cramped galley. Boone deputized me, but I'm not one of them. Not really. Outsider. Daughter of the town judge. I feel their skepticism like heat on the back of my neck.

Down a dark hallway, Clay emerges from a stateroom. "Look what I found," he says, dangling a pink leash from gloved hands for the deputies to see. His grin drops when his eyes land on me. "You again."

My stomach knots. I push through the crowd until I'm nose to nose with him. "Give me that." I snatch the leash, slip it into an evidence bag, and seal it shut.

Leaning past him, I glance into the stateroom. Nobody else is in there, nothing is out of place. I look back at Clay. "Well, isn't this convenient? You arrange a warrant with your buddy, the judge, and you're the one who finds the so-called murder weapon. What's next, Clay? You gonna pull Addie's ring out of your pocket?"

His grin twists into a snarl. "You've always had a smart

mouth. Funny thing is, it never gets you anywhere. Maybe you should let the men handle this."

The deputies go still, waiting for me to bite. I don't want a fight—not here, not while I'm holding the bag with the weapon that killed my best friend. But if I back down, I lose face, and I can't afford that. I'm already an outsider, still proving myself.

I meet his eyes, cold as a gun barrel. "You can try. But it'll be a woman who brings you down."

A low chuckle ripples through the group, deputies unable to hide their smirks. The sound dies the instant Boone steps into the doorway. His gaze sweeps the room, hard enough to knock the air flat. "What's going on in here?"

I hold the bagged leash out to Boone. "This, Sheriff. Right place, right time—almost like Clay knew exactly where to look." I feel Clay's eyes burning a hole in my back, but I don't dare turn around.

Boone's still studying the leash when voices rise outside—angry, urgent. Boots pound across the stern, and Ben bursts into the cabin, breathless, face flushed. His eyes dart from the deputies bagging evidence to the leash in Boone's hands. "What the hell are you doing on my boat?"

Boone squares his shoulders. "Ben Holloway, you're under arrest."

Ben's mouth falls open. "For what? For owning a dog leash?"

Clay shoves past me, knocking me off-balance. "This particular leash is the murder weapon. You killed my wife, you prick." He lunges for Ben, and deputies pounce, dragging him back.

"Cuff him, Sutherlin," Boone barks, holding out a pair of handcuffs.

I freeze, imagining the optics—the crowd outside, phones raised, snapping pictures of me hauling Tidewell's much-loved native son away in handcuffs. I'll be the villain. The headline. The outsider who put cuffs on one of their own.

I shove the cuffs back at Boone. "No way. Not me. This is Clay's rodeo. Let him do the honors."

Boone's jaw tightens, his eyes hard as granite. "I said cuff him, Sutherlin. That's an order."

The room goes still. Deputies look at me, waiting. Clay smirks in the corner, feeding on my hesitation. Ben's eyes plead with me, desperate, betrayed.

I don't have a choice. Not if I want to keep this badge. Not if I want to stay in this fight.

Forcing a breath, I snatch the handcuffs and step toward Ben. "Hands behind your back."

Ben shakes his head, backing toward the door. "Lane—please. Don't you turn on me too."

I lower my voice so only he can hear. "For now, we have no choice but to play along. But trust me, Ben. I will sort this out."

His voice cracks, half fury, half desperation. "You know I didn't hurt her."

"I know," I whisper. "I've got your back."

I've known this man all my life. The guy who offered me half his peanut butter sandwich in kindergarten. The guy who fixed my flat tire in the Food Lion parking lot, grease up to his elbows, grinning like it was nothing. The guy who still checks in on Mama Jean whenever her porch light burns too long.

The cuffs click shut, loud in the cramped cabin. On my way out, I glimpse Clay leaning against the galley counter, smug, watching the scene unfold exactly the way he wanted.

As I guide Ben up the narrow dock, I see the crowd spilling into the parking lot—neighbors, customers, gawkers—phones lifted, snapping pictures. Just as I feared. I'm the outsider, the villain, parading one of Tidewell's most honest men in handcuffs.

I don't have a cruiser, so I signal to Deputy Harrell. He takes Ben's arm, leading him toward the backseat of his waiting unit.

Ben twists to look at me, voice cracking. "I didn't do this, Lane. You know I'd never hurt her. I loved her. I never stopped loving her."

I fall in step, keeping my voice low. "Wait until we get to the station. You can tell me everything then."

Ben glances back, his eyes desperate. He gives a tight nod before ducking into the car.

I cling to that look all the way to the station, rehearsing the questions, imagining the dam finally breaking.

But by the time he's booked and led into the interview room, his expression has hardened. He lowers into the chair, shackled hands folded. "I'm not talking until I get a lawyer. But those bastards in booking won't let me use the phone."

My gut clenches. "What? Why not?"

His laugh is hollow. "Because in Tidewell, justice depends on which side of the line you stand. And I just got shoved to the wrong side." When his gaze lifts, the fight's gone from his face— only betrayal remains, raw and quiet. "These are all Clay's cronies. Sit tight, Lane. Tension's been brewing for years—and Clay just pulled the pin."

Boone warned me. Trina warned me. Heck, even Clay warned me. And now I can feel it for myself—the dark current is rising, threatening to pull us all under.

Chapter Twenty-Two

I'm relieved to see Lally's car still in the driveway when I pull in at five thirty. I'm neck-deep in this investigation, and I can't guarantee I'll be home by five every night. Lally's already doing more than her share. I can't ask her to cover weekends too.

My mind drifts to the fifty grand sitting in my bank account—the bail money we raised but never used. Maybe I can use some of it to hire some help, to buy us all a little breathing room.

My apologies precede me into the house. "I'm so sorry, Lally. I got tied up at work."

"I heard," Lally says, wiping her hands on a dish towel. "I'm so sorry about poor Ben Holloway. There's no way he hurt Addie. I remember how head over heels they were back in the day."

I brace myself for the warning everyone seems intent on giving me. But it doesn't come.

Lally pulls the apron over her head. "Did you get Ben released on bail?"

I shake my head. "Unfortunately, I don't think Ben's going anywhere anytime soon. Not until I find the real killer." Scout presses against my leg, and I lean down to hug her. I look back up at Lally. "I'm going to be busy with this case for a while. I should probably hire your niece. Can you have her stop by in the morning?"

"Yes, of course. That's a smart move." She smiles faintly. "You need to keep your mind on solving Addie's murder."

She grabs her purse from the laundry closet. "The judge is in his study, snoozing when I looked in on him a minute ago. I left you a chicken and rice casserole for your dinner."

I walk her to the back door. "Bless you, Lally. I don't know what we'd do without you."

"I'm glad to help. I only wish I could do more."

I press my cheek to hers. "You're doing plenty. Thank you."

Closing the door behind her, I look down at Scout, tail wagging and eyes hopeful. "Someone has some energy. Poor girl, been cooped up all day. Let me just check on the judge, then we'll play ball."

She trots along beside me as I poke my head into Dad's study —still napping. After checking that the front door's locked, I slide a decorative chair in front of it. The chair won't keep him in, but maybe it'll slow him down if he tries to wander.

Locating a tennis ball in the mudroom, I leave the French doors open so I can listen for Dad, and head outside with the dog. Scout bounds after the ball, ears flopping, tail high. We're only a few throws in when a door slams inside and heavy boots thud across the hardwoods.

Judd fills the doorway, chest heaving. "There you are. Thank God, you're okay."

I scrunch up my face. "I appreciate your concern, but why wouldn't I be?"

He pulls out his phone and scrolls, flashing the screen at me— shots of me in various angles, walking a handcuffed Ben from his boat to the cruiser. "I'm not saying it's your fault, but half this town's already decided you're the villain. Camp Ben—basically everybody—is furious you arrested him. Camp Clay's smaller but louder and way more powerful." He wiggles the phone. "Thanks to these posts, you're officially the most despised person in Tidewell."

I roll my eyes and push the phone away. "You're being melodramatic."

"I wish I were, Lane. I've already lost one sibling. I don't want to lose another. I prayed Addie would come home safe and sound so you could walk away before Tidewell's corruption swallowed you whole. But here you are, front and center. Wylie Craddock and Clay Dalton are bad news." He shakes his head. "Quit this investigation. Go back to Richmond, where you'll be safe."

Something icy snakes its way through my veins. *Wylie Craddock.* A name I'd hoped was locked in my past for good. "What's Wylie got to do with any of this?"

"Wylie has everything to do with everything. He runs this town—drugs, gambling, smuggling through the marina, squeezing business owners for protection money." Judd snatches up the tennis ball and hurls it toward the river. "Wylie's a modern-day mobster, and Clay Dalton's his right-hand man. I'm serious, Lane. Walk away before it's too late."

"Okay! Calm down, Judd, before you blow a gasket. I can't leave until the real killer's behind bars. But you don't need to worry about me. I'm a trained professional—I can take care of myself."

He sighs, bending to take the ball from Scout. "Look, I know Addie was your best friend, and you want justice for her, but—"

I cut him off. "It's not just about Addie anymore. She was pregnant. I have to solve this murder."

He doesn't speak for a long minute, then sinks into a lounge chair, the air punching out of him. "Wow. That's a game changer. Clay's a bastard, but he wouldn't kill an innocent unborn child—even if it wasn't his?"

I narrow my eyes. "What aren't you saying? You sound awfully sure it isn't his?"

"I'm not positive. But I've got a hunch." He falls back in the chair, dragging his fingers through his hair. "About nine months ago, Brandy and I went to Richmond to see a fertility specialist." His hand shoots up before I can speak. "And before you start asking questions, everything's fine with us. There's no medical reason she hasn't conceived." He lowers his hand. "Anyway, we ran into Clay and Addie in the waiting room. Clay looked like he wanted the floor to swallow him whole."

I motion for him to speed it up. "Get to the point, Judd."

"Maybe they were just there for her. But usually both partners get tested—like Brandy and me." He exhales, shoulders sagging. "If Addie was pregnant, the problem wasn't with her. Which means Ben is the baby daddy."

My throat tightens. "But you don't have any hard evidence they were having an affair."

"You want hard evidence?" Judd pulls out his phone and swipes to a photo of Ben, his face twisted in anguish. "There it is. Look at him, Lane. That man is hurting."

I let out a long sigh. "I know. I was with him this afternoon. He's devastated—going on and on about how much he loved Addie. Broke my heart."

When my gaze drifts toward the house, I see Dad standing in the doorway in his boxer shorts, his face twisted in confusion.

I rush toward him. "Dad! What're you doing?"

He shoves past me, stepping onto the bluestone in bare feet. "I need to get to my boat. I have to help Tommy."

Judd and I exchange a look. This is not a situation my training prepared me for.

I grab Dad's arm, but he jerks free, stronger than I expect, his bare feet slapping against the stone.

"Tommy keeps diving—over and over into the water—he's gotta get to the girl. She's down there. She's—" His voice breaks into a mumble, words slipping away.

My stomach drops. A girl? What girl?

"Dad, come on," Judd says gently, stepping in to block him. "Let's go back inside."

But Dad's fists ball, and he swings wildly, nearly catching Judd in the jaw. "No! Wylie said—Wylie said—" The rest tangles into a slur of syllables we can't make out.

I rest a reassuring hand on his shoulder. "Easy now, Dad. You don't have to help Tommy. He's safe."

He thrashes once more, then stumbles. Judd and I catch him under the arms and guide him up the steps.

His muttering fades to broken fragments. "Tommy . . . the girl . . . Wylie . . ."

By the time we ease him into his chair in the study, sweat beads at his temples. His chest heaves, eyelids drooping as the confusion pulls him under again.

I drag Judd to the far corner of the study, lowering my voice. "Did you know about a girl?"

His brow furrows. "No! I've never heard of a girl being mentioned before."

We trade a look—equal parts fear and dread.

"Maybe he's hallucinating," I suggest. "That can happen with Alzheimer's."

"Maybe." But his tone says he's not buying it.

The sound of running water filters in from down the hall. I stiffen. "Where's that coming from?"

Before I can go investigate, Dad stirs awake. He frowns, staring at his bare legs. "Where are my clothes? Why am I in my boxers?"

Judd and I exchange another look before I slip into the powder room. The sink is running, steam curling into the air, water circling the open drain. Dad's pants and shirt lie crumpled on the tile.

I shut off the tap, the silence pressing in heavy. Something about all this feels wrong—not just forgetful, but so very strange.

When I return to the study, Dad is dressed and acting like nothing happened. "What's for dinner? I'm starving?"

I chuckle at the absurdity of this disease—out of his mind one minute, fine the next. "Chicken and rice casserole à la Lally." I glance at my brother. "Can you stay?"

"I guess." Judd seems as reluctant to leave as he does to stay. Is he shaken by Dad's behavior—or by something else?

Instead of offering to help in the kitchen, he sits on the floor, playing with Scout. And while we eat, his mind is as far away as Dad's was a short while ago.

Dad, meanwhile, is sharp and animated as he discusses the dinner parties he's planning to host during the holidays. I can't help but wonder if he's even still in touch with half the people he's naming.

Over bowls of vanilla ice cream, I circle back to the question that's been eating at me. "Briggs is working on getting the charges dropped. Your name's on the guest log at Oyster Bay Estates, and Roxie admitted—begrudgingly—that you were there. I still haven't figured out why you'd go to her about your health. Did she help?"

"No," he says, voice as soft as the ripple of waves against the dock. "I can't explain it, Laney Bug. For some reason, despite everything we've been through, I keep expecting more of her. And she never fails to disappoint."

Dad's gaze travels to Judd. Something passes between them— old hurt and unfinished business.

Why can't love be enough? Why do we weigh it down with expectations until it collapses under the strain?

I'm surprised when Judd doesn't bolt after dinner. Something's on his mind, but he's waiting for the right moment to bring it up. While I do the dishes, he helps Dad get ready for bed. I'm outside with Scout, the sun now a fading orange memory, when he joins me with two lowball glasses—one chunk of ice, two fingers of whiskey.

"How much do you remember about the accident?" he asks, the words thick in his throat.

Here we go. I take a sip of bourbon, needing the liquid courage to revisit the past—that fateful Fourth of July, nineteen years ago. "Some parts are a blur, but others I remember like they happened yesterday. I spent much of that day with Mama Jean and Addie. A few of our friends' families were camped down the beach from the party. We planned to stay for the fireworks, then Mama Jean got a call. Said there'd been an emergency, and we needed to leave.

"In hindsight, Mama Jean must have told Addie. The ride home was eerie—no chatter, no music, just silence pressing in from every side. Only the hum of the tires and the weight of a storm I couldn't yet see. I knew something terrible had happened. I felt the loss before I understood it."

I take another sip of bourbon, welcoming the burn as it steels my nerves. "When we got home, Lally was already there. I don't know where Dad was. Mom just blurted out the news—no sugar-coating it—that Tommy had been killed in a boating accident. I remember being terrified about you. I didn't know where you were, or if something bad had happened to you too. I lost it—screaming and crying. Someone called old Dr. Jenkins, or maybe he just stopped by. I'm not sure. But he gave me a shot that knocked me out cold."

I pause, letting the silence stretch before I ask, "So where were you—and why have we never talked about this?"

He shakes his head. "Dad said we couldn't. Don't ask me why. Just another mystery about that awful day." He drains his glass in one swallow. "I was at Jake's. His parents were out of town, and we were having a raging party. I was too drunk to come home when Mom called. Brandy took care of me. She's been taking care of me since."

I never particularly cared for Brandy, but this softens me toward her. She picked up the pieces when the rest of us fell apart.

Judd buries his face in his hands. His voice comes muffled. "I never understood why Wylie Craddock was with Tom that day. They hated each other. I've always suspected he had something to do with Tom's death—that maybe it wasn't an accident. And what about the girl Dad mentioned? Who was she? Why are we only hearing about her now?"

Judd's the only one who ever called our older brother *Tom*.

Hearing it now lands like a fist in my stomach. "Dad has Alzheimer's, Judd. You saw him—he barely knew where he was. Like I said earlier, he was probably hallucinating."

Judd lifts his head, his dark eyes boring into me. "But what if he wasn't?"

The night air grows heavier, Scout snoring softly at my feet. I want to dismiss it—chalk it up to Dad's broken mind—but Judd's words have lodged deep. For the first time, I wonder if the fragments spilling from my father's lips aren't madness at all but pieces of a truth no one wanted me to find.

Across the water, a buoy bell tolls—low and hollow—the sound echoing like a warning.

Chapter Twenty-Three

I open my eyes Wednesday morning to find Scout staring at me, legs tucked beneath her, head resting on the pillow beside mine. I touch my nose to hers. "That's it—we're officially a couple. But we've got to do something about that breath."

Rolling onto my back, I stare at the ceiling as last night comes rushing back. Dad in his boxers, rambling on about some mysterious girl who was with Tommy the night of the accident. Judd and me on the patio, finally unpacking that dreadful night. And then—Judd mentioning seeing Addie and Clay at the fertility specialist in Richmond.

I bolt upright, grab my phone from the nightstand, and punch in my brother's number.

Judd answers on the second ring, voice thick with sleep. "Ugh. Why are you calling so early?"

I glance at the clock on my nightstand. "It's seven o'clock. Time to get up. What's the name of the fertility specialist in Richmond?"

"I forgot," he says—too quick, too flat.

"Then ask Brandy," I snap.

"Leave it alone, Lane. We don't want to get involved."

"If you don't tell me, I'll sic Boone on you."

Sheets rustle on the other end. Then—nothing. The line stays quiet for so long I think he's hung up. "Judd?"

"Dr. Margaret Ellison," he mutters at last. "But leave us out of it. If Clay Dalton comes after me or Brandy, I'm holding you personally responsible."

"We never had this conversation. I promise."

Ending the call, I roll onto my side, facing Scout, stroking her head. "What do you think, girl? Up for a road trip to Richmond?"

Her tail thumps once against the mattress.

"I'll take that as a yes." I throw back the covers. "We'd better get moving."

On the way to the bathroom, I peek in on Dad—still sleeping soundly. But when I get out of the shower, his bed is empty. Heart pounding, I yank on jeans and a lightweight sweater, Scout bounding after me as I race downstairs.

Relief floods me when I find him in the kitchen with Lally and an attractive stranger who must be her niece.

"Morning, Dad." I kiss his cheek, then turn to the woman, offering my hand. "I'm Lane. Thanks for coming."

"Of course." Her grip is firm, her smile warm. Up close, she appears to be in her mid-thirties—young for someone running a caregiver service. "I'm Hannah Price. Nice to finally meet you."

Lally presses a warm mug of coffee into my hands. "Here. Looks like you need this."

I chuckle. "Do the bags under my eyes give me away?"

She cups my cheek, her palm soft and cool. "You're lovely as ever. Just have a lot on your plate."

"True that." I shift my gaze back to Hannah, nodding toward the French doors. "I need to take the dog out. If you don't mind, we can talk outside."

We step onto the patio, and Scout trots off to nose the pansies. I gesture toward the wrought-iron chairs. "Shall we sit?"

"I wish I could." Regret flickers behind Hannah's warm smile. "Your view is lovely. I could stay here all morning. Unfortunately, I'm short on time." She blows on her coffee before taking a sip.

"Lally has talked about the judge so much over the years, I feel like I already know him. It's a shame what's happening."

Through the window, I watch Dad at the table, working the crossword in today's newspaper. "Sometimes he seems perfectly normal. Then, in an instant, he turns into someone I don't recognize."

"Alzheimer's is an ugly disease," she says quietly, following my gaze.

I catch myself, not wanting to scare her off. "He's really no trouble, though. We just have to keep an eye on him so he doesn't wander. I need someone here in the evenings after Lally leaves, and on weekends—at least until I wrap up this murder investigation. Then we'll reassess."

What happens when I go back to Richmond? *If* I go back to Richmond? Can we afford round-the-clock care? Even the best caregivers need direction. Can I really count on Judd to manage things?

Hannah's expression softens. "I knew Addie—not well. Our paths only crossed once in a blue moon. But she lit up every room she entered. Tidewell's darker without her." Her gaze holds mine, her eyes fierce. "Catch the bastard who did this."

I nod, throat tight. "That's the plan."

"Don't worry about your dad. I've got you covered. Shall we start today?"

Hope flares in my chest. "Can you? That'd be great. I'm heading to Richmond to track down a lead. I may be late getting back."

"Not a problem. But you need to be patient. It might take a week or so to sort things out, to find the right fit for the judge."

I walk her to the door, Scout padding alongside us. There's a quiet strength about Hannah I didn't expect—no-nonsense, yet kind. Exactly what we need. For the first time in days, I feel like I can leave Dad without looking over my shoulder.

———

The fertility specialist's office sits in a bland medical building off Glen Forest Drive in Richmond. The moment I step inside, the air feels charged, almost humming. The waiting room is empty—no patients, no chatter, just the staccato clack of keyboards and the clipped tones of staff in blue scrubs on the phones behind the reception desk, working with a frantic energy that makes my skin prickle.

They don't even look up when I walk in. I clear my throat, and finally a young woman with blonde braids and a phone pressed to her ear flicks her gaze my way. She lifts a finger, mouthing, "Just a minute."

I can't help but catch her end of the conversation. She's canceling a patient's appointment, offering no explanation beyond, "The doctor isn't available today."

When the caller presses, her tone tightens. "I'm sorry, but I don't know when Dr. Ellison will be able to see you. Would you like me to refer you to another specialist?"

The hairs on the back of my neck rise. Something is definitely off.

Blonde Braids slams down the phone and looks up at me, exasperated. Her gaze shifts to Scout, then back. "Dogs aren't allowed in here."

"She's a service dog." I flash my badge. "I need to speak with Dr. Ellison about one of her patients."

Her chin drops to her chest, a hand covering her eyes. "I'm sorry. The doctor is . . ." A sob slips out. "Dead!"

Two women circle her, rubbing her back. She's not the first to break down today. It's clear Dr. Ellison's death was sudden.

An older woman with a severe dark bun steps forward. "What do you want?" she snaps. "Can't you see we're busy here?"

"I'm Detective Lane Sutherlin." I hold out my badge again. "What happened to Dr. Ellison? If you don't mind me asking."

"I *do* mind. What can I help you with, Detective?"

"I'm working a murder investigation down in Tidewell that involves one of Dr. Ellison's patients."

Her body tenses, her shoulders squared. "And?"

"I need some information. Her name was Addie Dalton. I need to know the nature of her infertility. The autopsy showed she was about eight weeks pregnant."

Blonde Braids gasps, her hand flying to her mouth.

The older woman says, "How tragic. I'm so sorry." She moves to the nearest computer, her fingers flying across the keyboard. "I don't see an Addie Dalton in our system. Are you sure you have the right fertility specialist? There are several in the city."

"I'm positive. I have firsthand knowledge she consulted with Dr. Ellison."

"If she's not in our system, there's nothing else I can do." The older woman answers a ringing phone, effectively dismissing me.

From behind a tissue, Blonde Braids sniffles. "Her name's familiar. Do you have a picture?"

I pull up Addie's Instagram account and slide the phone across the counter.

She scrolls, then stops, tapping on a picture of Clay. "I remember now. Hard to forget a face like that—perfect teeth and a rotten soul. He hit on me—totally inappropriate on about five different levels."

I roll my eyes. Only Clay would hit on a nurse while accompanying his wife to a fertility clinic.

I nod toward the computer. "Will you check again, please?" I glance at her name tag. "Chloe."

She gives me a quick nervous smile before dropping into her chair and craning her neck toward the screen. She types for several minutes before looking up again, her expression grim. "I don't see her name anywhere. This is very strange."

An uneasy ripple stirs in my gut. "How did you say Dr. Ellison died again?"

Her face tightens. "I didn't. She was—"

Before she can finish, the outer door bangs open, rattling the glass. A stream of Richmond police officers flood the office, boots thudding against the tile. I recognize several faces. And bringing up the rear—Milo and Amanda.

Seeing me, Amanda's face lights up, and she makes a beeline over. "Thank goodness you're back. The department's been a circus without you. Milo thinks he's in charge—barking orders like he's the chief." She glances down at Scout. "And who's your adorable sidekick?"

"This is Scout." I grin down at her as she wags her tail.

Amanda smile fades. "Wait—I'm confused. Aren't you still on leave? I thought Morales gave you a month."

"He did. But I'm temporarily working a murder investigation." My throat tightens. Amanda knows Addie is—*was*—my best friend. She's heard me talk about her for years. I pull her aside, lowering my voice. "The victim was Addie. I insisted on being part of the investigation."

Her hand flies to her mouth. "Addie? Your best friend since birth, Addie?"

I nod, unable to speak.

"Oh, Lane. I'm so sorry." She throws her arms around me. "That's awful."

I let out a gush of air. "I still can't believe it."

Amanda eases back. "I remember now—Scout was Addie's dog."

I rub Scout's head. "Yep. We've adopted each other."

Confusion knits her brow. "Why are you here if you're investigating a murder in Tidewell?"

"Tracking down a lead. Allegedly, Addie was a patient of Dr. Ellison, but her name's mysteriously vanished from their system." I jab a finger at her. "Your turn. Why are *you* here? How did Ellison die?"

"Home invasion," she says quietly. "At first, we thought it was random . . ."

A shiver crawls up my spine. "But . . . ?"

"Her house was ransacked, but according to her husband,

nothing appears to be missing—no jewelry, no electronics, no cash."

"Where was the husband at the time?"

"On a red-eye from Los Angeles. We've confirmed with the airline—he's not a suspect. He found her when he got home this morning." Amanda's eyes glisten, and she looks away. "Poor man was wrecked. I felt so sorry for him."

Cold settles in my bones. Random, my foot. Someone wanted Margaret Ellison silenced. But who—and why? And what does any of this have to do with Addie? If anything.

Milo saunters over. "Sutherlin." His eyes rake me up and down. "Still skinny. Still haggard. I thought Morales sent you home to Daddy to rest. What're you doing here?"

My gaze drifts from the slick shine of his hair to the smug polish of his loafers. "Milo. Still slimy. Still shady. And I'm working. Same as you."

He snaps his fingers. "That's right—I heard you lost an old friend."

My stomach knots. *I knew it!* He's the varmint who ratted me out to Clay. I force a tight smile. "Old friend—something you'll never have."

His face beams red, and I resist the urge to say, *gotcha.*

I turn back to Amanda. "Walk me out?" I say, heading for the door without waiting for her response.

Milo mutters something under his breath as I brush past him, but I don't bother asking him to repeat it. If there's one thing I've learned about Milo Sanchez, it's that he thrives on attention. Best thing I can do is starve him of it.

Amanda catches up with me outside in the hallway. "Lane, you're gonna regret making enemies of Milo . . ."

"I'm not worried about Milo." I throw her a glance over my shoulder. "Do me a favor. Check with whoever's running the scene at Ellison's. See if any keys are missing. Or a notebook—something she might've used for passwords."

"Why? What're you getting at?"

We pause beside the elevator. "Just a hunch." I hold her gaze, willing her to trust me. "If I'm right, I'll explain later."

She exhales, glancing back toward the office like Milo might slither through the door at any second. "I shouldn't . . . but I will. Only because your hunches have a habit of being right."

Warmth pricks my throat. I lean close, pressing a cheek to hers. "Thanks. I owe you one," I whisper.

Behind us, Milo clears his throat—loud, performative. I don't give him the satisfaction of looking back as I step inside the elevator.

Chapter Twenty-Four

On the way out of town, I swing by my apartment to grab more clothes. The air has turned crisp, and I need sweaters and jackets.

When I open the door, stale air greets me, heavy and close. I pause just inside, taking in what I've been ignoring for months—the dingy walls, the water stain spreading like a bruise across the ceiling, the view of that same ugly red brick building pressing against my window. No wonder I never felt at home here.

My mind drifts to my family's home on River Birch Farm, with its shady oaks and soft furnishings—the kind of place that breathes warmth into you. This place? It's just four walls. I never lived here, only existed, moving through each day on autopilot. I can't remember the last time I stopped to notice anything good—not since I started suspecting Grayson's affair.

Scout presses against my legs with a low whine.

"I know, girl. It's bad." I scratch behind her ears. "You're the only bright spot in this dingy place. Give me a minute to pack, and we'll walk through the park before heading back. Some fresh air will do us both good."

She slinks to the door and flops down with a sigh, as if afraid I might leave her behind in this awful apartment.

I fill three duffel bags with the rest of my clothes, then empty the refrigerator of its moldy offerings. The motions feel final, like closing the cover on a book I never should've opened. Deep down, I know I won't be coming back. This apartment was never home—just a stepping stone. Richmond itself was only a chapter, a stop on my journey of life.

I slip on a pair of old running shoes and clip Scout's leash. Byrd Park will be the only thing I miss about Richmond—the lakes dotted with geese, the steady stream of joggers, the easy rhythm of people walking their dogs.

The night Addie disappeared was the last time I came here. I lay down in the grass and cried—over my wreck of a life, over my suspension from Richmond PD, over the breakup of my marriage. All the while, my best friend was living her last hours. Fixing her husband dinner. Walking her dog one final time.

Then what, Addie? Where did you go? Ben's houseboat? Did you break the news about the pregnancy? Or did he already know? Did you know who the father was?

The questions thud in my chest with every step. Only one scenario makes sense. And to prove it, I need Addie's medical records from Dr. Ellison.

I'm loading my bags in my car thirty minutes later when my phone buzzes in my pocket. Amanda's name lights the screen.

"Lane, you were right," she says without preamble. "Keys are missing from Ellison's house."

A chill slides down my spine. "Keys to her office?"

"Yep. And there's something else." Amanda lowers her voice. "Apparently, Ellison's entire database was wiped clean—records, backups, everything. Our tech guys are on it, but they're not hopeful about recovering much."

I slam the hatch shut and lean against the bumper. Whoever broke in wasn't just snooping—they knew exactly what they were doing. "Any idea when it happened?"

"Hard to say. The timestamp's been scrubbed too."

My pulse quickens. That takes serious skill—and serious motive. Someone wanted Ellison's work to disappear.

"You didn't hear it from me," Amanda mutters.

"Understood. I owe you one."

"Lane?" Her voice softens. "Be careful. After you left, Milo was asking a lot of questions about your relationship with Addie. I don't know why he'd even be interested, but he is. Just . . . watch your back."

Her words leave a bitter taste in my mouth. Of course Milo's sniffing around Addie. News of my suspension didn't land in Clay's lap by accident. Those two are clearly working together.

The drive back to Tidewell blurs by in a haze of racing thoughts. This wasn't some amateur break-in. Someone professionally wiped Ellison's entire database—every record, every backup. This is bigger than Addie's fertility issues, and Clay Dalton's covering his tracks like a cat in a litter box. Coincidence? My gut says no. One thing's for certain. I can't afford to wait for answers to surface on their own.

By the time I turn off the highway toward Tidewell, the sun is sliding toward evening. Too late to search Clay's house today. Neighbors will be out walking dogs, kids pedaling bikes. If I try to slip inside now, I'll draw every eye on the block. It'll have to wait until morning.

I grip the wheel tighter, frustration burning hotter than my headlights. Every minute wasted feels like handing Clay more time to cover his tracks.

The fog gathers low as I approach the bridge, curling off the water in ghostly ribbons. Scout stirs in the back, giving a soft whine that prickles my nerves even more.

Halfway across, headlights flare in my rearview mirror—high, bright, bearing down too fast. A truck—a dark color, black or charcoal grey, with jacked-up tires. I ease right to let it pass, but instead, it swerves with me, riding my bumper so close I can't see the grille.

The first tap jolts my car forward, metal on metal. My heart leaps to my throat. The second hit comes harder, a deliberate shove that sends me skidding toward the guardrail. Scout yelps, claws scrambling against the seat.

I wrench the wheel, tires screaming, fighting for control. My breath rasps loud in my ears. Whoever's behind the wheel isn't careless—they're trying to kill me.

Instinct kicks in, and my hand flies to the console. Empty. My gun isn't there. I'd locked it up for safety in case Dad stumbled across it.

The truck surges alongside, window down. I force my eyes sideways just long enough to glimpse the driver before he speeds off. Recognition slams into me like the impact itself. *Wylie Craddock*. And he wanted me to see him.

I should call the police. Then I remember—I am the police. Currently, the only ethical branch of the Tidewell Sheriff's Office.

I've been threatened, chased, even shot at. But having someone try to ram me off a bridge is a new one. I'm too shaken to go after him, and I don't dare stop on the bridge to survey the damage.

Taking deep breaths to calm the wild hammering in my chest, I cross the bridge with white-knuckled hands gripping the wheel, turning onto Tidewater Drive toward the farm.

In the driveway, I park and sweep my flashlight over the Bronco's rear end. The bumper's crumpled. Perfect. I will send Wylie Craddock the bill.

Entering the house, I find Dad pacing while a young caregiver hovers near tears. She can't be more than eighteen. Why would Hannah send someone so green? My mind flashes to the bridge, to Wylie's truck. Was he here too? Did he threaten Dad?

My heart pounding in my throat, I look from Dad to the girl and back. "What's going on? Did something happen?"

"Make this woman leave," Dad barks, voice booming with the courtroom authority I grew up with. "She's been on me like stink on a skunk all afternoon. She even stood outside the bathroom door while I peed."

"That's not true." The caregiver snatches up her purse. "He's impossible. He doesn't need a caregiver. He needs a prison guard." She storms out, the door rattling in her wake.

"Dad, that wasn't very nice," I scold, sharper than I intend.

"I don't need a babysitter, Lane."

"Are you sure about that? We can't afford to have you wandering off again. Remember the last time you had murder charges brought against you?"

His glare is all fire, but behind it, the confusion churns. He doesn't remember. "I don't know what you're talking about."

I press my lips together, swallowing the retort burning my tongue. "Let's get you some supper. Want to cook something?"

"No," he says, arms folded tight like a child refusing bedtime.

"Well, I'm starving." I root through the fridge, forcing cheer. "Soup. Grilled cheese. Leftover spaghetti." I check the oven. "Ooh —Lally left fried chicken. I'll throw together a salad."

"I'm not hungry."

"But you love Lally's chicken."

He gives his head a vehement shake. "I do not."

"Then let's have a glass of wine first," I say, removing a bottle from the wine rack. He doesn't need alcohol. He needs something stronger, real medication. But desperate times call for desperate measures.

Dad doesn't eat, but he seems to enjoy the wine. Within the hour, he's calm enough for me to get him into bed.

Back in the kitchen, Scout gazes up at me with those warm brown eyes. "What is it, girl?" Then it hits me—I forgot to feed her dinner.

I fill her bowl, watching her dive in, then slip outside with my phone. Hannah's name glows on the screen as I press call.

She answers on the first ring. "Lane! I just heard what happened. I'm so sorry. Normally, I spend the first few days with a new client to get a feel for things. But I have a difficult case right now—an old client on her deathbed."

"It's my fault, Hannah. I wasn't entirely truthful this morning.

Dad can sometimes be a handful. Lessons learned for us both. We're going to need someone with more experience."

A pause stretches on the other end. "Shawna *is* my most experienced CNA."

"Really? She looks so young."

Hannah chuckles softly. "Don't let looks fool you. She's almost forty, and she's highly capable." Another pause. "Has the judge seen a doctor lately? He might benefit from something to help him through the sundown hours."

"No, but that's a good idea. I'm on it."

We say our goodbyes, and I slip the phone back into my pocket. But the conversation lingers long after the call ends. Dad should have seen a doctor months ago. But Judd sat on it, and now the burden is mine.

I lean against the porch railing, the night closing in around me as I replay my day. Meeting with Hannah. Trip to Richmond. Ellison's death. Nearly run off a bridge by Wylie Craddock. And here I am, ending the day the same way I began it—trying to hold together a father who's slipping further from me by the hour.

Scout noses my hand, her steady warmth pulling me back from the edge. I give her a pat. "We'll figure it out, girl," I whisper. But the words taste hollow.

Because tonight, I'm not sure how much more either of us can take.

Chapter Twenty-Five

The night is fractured with dreams that drag me back years —Wylie's hand pinning me down, his vicious laughter in my ear, the stink of his breath. I thrash awake, heart hammering, sweat soaking the sheets.

Scout whines at the foot of the bed, ears pricked. That's when I hear it too—shrill, insistent, cutting through the dark. *The house alarm.* For a split second, I think I'm still dreaming. Then the realization—Dad left the house.

I'm out of bed and flying down the stairs, two at a time, Scout on my heels. The front door gapes wide open, but Dad is nowhere in sight.

I'm tempted to go after him in bare feet and pajamas, but reason wins out—I'll be more effective if I get shoes and a light. Dashing back inside, I jam my feet into running shoes, grab my phone off the nightstand, and bolt back out into the night.

I hesitate at the end of the sidewalk. Car or foot? I can cover more ground in the car, but on foot, I can check the places he might hide. Halfway down the quarter-mile drive, I realize my mistake. Dad could be knocking on the door of the governor's mansion in Richmond by now. Still, I push toward the road. With no sign of him in either direction, I turn and retrace my steps to the house.

Loading Scout into the car, we speed down to the waterfront. After a fruitless search of the cottage, I head for the dock—and freeze. A faint light flickers on the stern of Dad's boat. My stomach drops.

I move in closer. He's standing at the edge, peering into the inky water, a propane lantern guttering beside him. One wrong move, and it'll topple—teak catching like kindling, the gas engine ready to blow.

Perfect. I survived Wylie trying to run me off a bridge, only to lose Dad to an explosion.

"Sit. Stay," I tell Scout, pointing to the grass. She drops obediently, eyes fixed on me, body taut with worry.

Slipping off my shoes, I moved toward the boat and step onboard, grabbing the lantern before Dad realizes I'm here.

"Dad?" I say softly. "What're you doing?"

He doesn't look up, his gaze locked on the black water. "Looking for Tommy. I can't let him drown again."

The words hit like a punch to the gut, stealing the air from my lungs.

"He was just here," he says, voice trembling. "I saw him go under."

"Tommy's not in the water, Dad." I tug gently on his sleeve. "Come inside with me."

His face crumples, but he lets me lead him off the boat. I extinguish the lantern and use my phone's flashlight to guide us down the dock to the car. He sinks into the passenger seat, shoulders slumped, sniffling—a broken man. My heart splinters into a million pieces.

Just when I think things can't get worse, they do.

———

Back inside the house, I reset the security alarm and settle Dad back to bed. It's already five o'clock. After the nightmare and his disappearance, sleep's out of the question. I take a long, hot shower to ease the tension in my muscles, then dress in jeans and a soft navy pullover.

I'm drinking coffee in the kitchen when Lally arrives at nine. "Hannah told me what happened yesterday," she says, tying an apron around her waist. "Shawna is highly capable, but despite her best efforts to calm him, I could tell the judge wasn't having it. I shouldn't have left him."

"You did the right thing, Lally. It was time for you to go home. This isn't your problem."

"Now, listen here, missy." She wags a finger at me. "We're all family here. You'd do the same thing for me."

Would I? I'm not so sure. "He's getting worse," I admit. "He got out during the night—early this morning, actually. I found him on his boat with a lantern, looking into the water for Tommy." A tear slides down my cheek. I swipe it away before it falls. "If he'd knocked the lantern over, he'd have blown both of us to smithereens."

Lally sinks onto the chair beside me, laying a warm hand on my back. "God bless you, child. I'm so sorry."

"What do I do, Lally? I can't be here with him all the time."

"Of course not. You have a very important job. Even if you didn't, it's not fair for you to shoulder this burden alone. Your daddy will eventually get used to having someone around. He just needs time."

"I hope you're right." I straighten, reaching for a napkin to blow my nose. "I'll try to be home before you leave this afternoon. Maybe my presence will make things a little less tense with the sitter."

"That's not a bad idea. But don't worry if you're running late. I can stay with him for a while."

"You're the best, Lally." My lips part in a tired smile. "By the way, thanks for the fried chicken. It was delicious as always." I push back from the counter. "I need to get to town."

"I'll fix you some breakfast to take with you."

I start to protest, but my stomach says otherwise.

While Lally whips up a scrambled egg sandwich, I feed Scout. When the dog tries to follow me out, I crouch down beside her. "I've got an important mission for you today. Keep an eye on the judge. If anything strange happens, you let Lally know. Deal?"

She wags her tail as though she understands.

I enjoy having her ride shotgun, but the first stop of the day is Clay's house, and I don't want to upset her when Addie's not there.

On the way to town, I call young Dr. Jenkins, namesake and successor to the doctor who was my pediatrician, the same doctor who medicated me the night of Tommy's accident. The Jenkins family has been tending Tidewell for generations—delivering babies, patching wounds, and burying the dead.

I'm disappointed when the receptionist tells me he can't see Dad for two weeks. Two weeks would be a miracle in New York City, but this is Tidewell, where a man like Dad shouldn't have to wait. I schedule the appointment anyway and ask to be put on the waitlist in case of a cancellation.

At the rate he's slipping, Dad could wander to Timbuktu before we see the doctor.

By the time I ease onto Clay's street a few minutes before ten, the sun is high in the sky, casting golden light across manicured lawns. Clay will have left for work a couple of hours ago. Broad daylight isn't the best time to play detective, but waiting isn't an option.

I park a block away and force myself to walk casually toward their house. I nod at a neighbor pruning roses as if I belong here, as if I have every right to stroll toward Clay's front walk. But my heart drums a warning, loud enough I'm sure the whole street can hear it.

I locate the hidden key under the potted plant on the back

porch—the first sign that what I'm looking for isn't here. Clay would never be this careless. But I have to rule out the possibility.

The lock gives with a soft click, and I slip inside, ears straining for any sound beyond the hush of the house. A wave of sour, rotting garbage hits me square in the face. Typical man—can't take care of a home to save his life.

I head straight for the study tucked into the far back corner. I move quickly through the desk, rifling drawers, flipping through folders. Insurance papers, tax returns—nothing that breathes, nothing that ties Clay to Addie's last days. The absence itself sets my teeth on edge. Too neat. Too bare. Like someone went through and scrubbed it all down to the bone. In the bottom right drawer, I discover a forgotten object that will definitely come in handy later. I slip it into my pocket and continue my search.

I swivel the chair to face the credenza behind it. The silver frame with the enamel daisies—white petals, yellow centers—still sits in its usual spot. But the photo inside is gone: the snapshot of Addie and me on graduation day, arms linked, sunburnt and smiling. I gave her that framed photo myself, and she's kept it here ever since. Until now.

The empty frame stares back at me like an accusation. Not just erasing Addie—erasing *us*. This isn't careless. It's intentional. A message from Clay. He knew I'd come looking.

I spring to my feet and bolt for the door, heart thrumming in my throat. What if it's not the house that's been staged—what if the trap is for me? The thought chases me down the hall and out onto the porch.

I freeze at the top of the steps. Wylie Craddock stands at the bottom, eyes drilling into me, all quiet arrogance and calculated control. The weight of my gun presses into the small of my back. I didn't forget today. I rarely make the same mistake twice.

The old fear hits hard and fast—the one Wylie branded into me years ago. My stomach churns, knees begging to buckle, but I lock them in place. He will *not* see me fold.

Wylie's mouth curls into a smirk, his voice low and oily.

"Looking for something, Lane? You should be more careful where you stick that pretty nose."

I meet his gaze. "I wasn't sticking my nose in anywhere, Wylie. Just looking for a leash for Scout. You wouldn't know where I might find one, would you? Maybe a pink one—with Scout's name embroidered in white?"

At the mention of the leash, Wylie's face pales, then his jaw hardens. "Careful, Lane. You keep pushing, you'll find yourself in deeper than you can climb out."

I step down onto the patio, chin high. "I've been in worse places. And I always climb out. You've seen it. You know."

I move to brush past him, but his hand shoots out, clamping around my arm. His grip is iron—the same grip from nineteen years ago. Bile rises in my throat. His breath, his laughter, all of it crashing back like a wave I can't outrun.

"Let go." My voice comes out like a growl.

He leans closer, eyes gleaming. "Maybe you like me holding on."

My knees go weak—what if I crumble? No, Lane! Not this time. You can't let him hurt you again.

I steel myself, let the rage burn hotter than the fear. "Get your hands off me." I yank my arm free, hard enough to make him stumble. "Touch me again, and I'll tell Tidewell exactly what you are."

I stride past him, pulse thundering.

He doesn't follow, but his voice carries after me—low and sharp as a knife. "Watch yourself, Lane. You don't know what you're up against."

Chapter Twenty-Six

Wylie's eyes burn a hole in my back as I walk away, but I resist the urge to flip him off. My hand grazes my pocket —key still there.

Focus, Sutherlin. You've got this.

I drive the short blocks to the town and park behind the sheriff's department. From the rear of the Bronco, I grab the backpack I keep for emergency ops. Inside the station, I nod to the desk agent and head straight for the locker room, thankful to find it empty.

Five minutes later, I emerge a blonde with a pixie cut, wearing a short dress that swishes around my thighs. Not exactly my style, but perfect for the job.

I swing by the Salty Bean—more to check my tail than to grab caffeine. The scent of espresso hangs heavy in the air, the low hum of gossip filling the space. As I wait in line, two women behind me debate whether Clay or Ben killed Addie.

I spin around, glare sharp enough to cut glass. "You're talking about a young woman's life, not a reality TV show."

One of them huffs, unimpressed.

The other shrugs. "We're just saying what everyone else in town is saying. It's Team Clay versus Team Ben—take your pick."

My blood boils. "Addie's not a ballgame. And this sure as hell isn't a team sport."

Their eyes widen, but I don't wait for a comeback. I place my order with a fake name, head down the hall toward the restroom, then slip out the back door.

I grip the key as I make my way down the block to Crown & Glory. Blue masking tape wrapped around the handle reads Salon, but I hold my breath anyway as I slide it into the lock. No alarm sounds. The hinges groan softly as I ease inside and head for the small office.

I drop into the desk chair and rifle through drawers. Invoices. Appointment logs. Each tab labeled in Addie's neat, looping handwriting. Nothing useful. Disappointment overcomes me. I shove the drawer closed—too hard. The wood catches with a sharp snap that echoes through the tiny office.

I lean back, scanning the cramped room—the humming mini fridge, the corkboard cluttered with faded reminders. Then my gaze snags on the framed certificate above the desk—Addie's cosmetology license, the gold seal dulled by time.

Something about it draws me closer, a crackle in the air as if the room itself is holding its breath. The frame lifts easily from the wall. My heart thunders as I turn it over.

What looks like the same blue painter's tape secures a thick envelope, pressed flat against the cardboard backing of the frame. My fingers tremble as I peel the tape away and slide the envelope out.

Clay's name stares back at me from the report header. I scan the page until one word leaps out, impossible to unsee—*infertile.*

I let out a low whistle. So Judd was right. *Usually both partners get tested . . . If Addie was pregnant, the problem wasn't with her.*

But this raises more questions than it answers. Why did Addie feel the need to hide the report—and why here, of all places? Did Clay not know the results? Was she afraid of how he'd react if he found out?

Infertility isn't the end of the world—it's not cancer—but for a man like Clay, it would be a devastating blow to his ego.

Or . . . what if she knew Ben was the father and wanted to pass the baby off as Clay's? That thought chills me.

The possibilities spiral, each one darker than the last. But for Addie's sake, I won't settle for speculation. I'll find the truth—whatever it costs.

One thing's for certain. Dr. Ellison didn't die *because* Clay Dalton is infertile. But my gut tells me the cases are connected. I need to figure out how. And I know just who to talk to.

Snapping a photo of the report, I slide it back into the envelope, press it flat against the frame's backing, and hang the license exactly as I found it. I sneak out the back door and retrace my steps to the coffee shop. A cup with my fake name on it still sits on the counter, the coffee now lukewarm.

I claim a small table in the corner, pull out my phone, and open Dr. Ellison's website. A quick scroll through the staff directory jogs my memory—Morgan. Chloe Morgan.

I could request her number from the phone company, but that's red tape I don't have time for.

A quick Instagram search takes me right to her profile—a picture of a smiling Chloe in pink scrubs holding a fluffy white cat. I hit *Message* and type: *This is Detective Lane Sutherlin. We met yesterday in Dr. Ellison's office. I have a few questions and would appreciate a call as soon as you can.*

I set the phone on the table and wait, pulse ticking with the rhythm of the espresso machine.

Five minutes later, I'm still staring at my screen, fiddling with the fine blonde hairs at the nape of my neck, wishing Chloe would respond, when a text from Boone flashes across the screen.

My office. Now!

"Seriously, Boone?" I mutter to the phone. "Your timing is impeccable."

I fire back a quick reply.

Be there in five.

Tossing my empty cup in the trash can, I dart into the restroom and peel off the wig. There's nothing I can do about the flimsy dress. It's too tight, too short, and way too revealing for a meeting with the sheriff, but I don't have time to change.

I'm hustling down Main Street when my phone rings—*unknown number*.

I slow my pace and answer. "Sutherlin."

"Detective? This is Chloe Morgan. Do you have news about Dr. Ellison's death?"

"I'm sorry, Chloe. I don't. But I do have questions about Dr. Ellison's treatment of Addie Dalton, and I was hoping you could help me."

"I can try. But patient confidentiality prevents me from saying too much."

I glance around, making sure no one is watching me, then lean casually against the post office wall. "The patient is dead, Chloe. I'm trying to find her killer. I'd hate to drag you all the way down to the sheriff's office in Tidewell, but I will if I have to. Everything you tell me is completely off the record."

A long silence stretches between us before she lets out a sigh of resignation. "Okay. She was such a sweet person. I really want you to find the person who killed her."

"Then help me."

Another pause. I hear her swallow on the other end, followed by a shaky breath. "Okay . . . let's see . . . I happened to answer the phone when Addie called, asking for her results."

"When was this?"

"Back in January—several weeks after her appointment." Chloe's voice softens. "That alone made me suspicious. It usually only takes a few days for results to come in. But when I checked, her chart was blank. No test results. No notes. Nothing."

I grip the phone tighter. "What did you do?"

"I told her I'd look into it and call her back. When I asked Dr. Ellison about the case, she brushed me off—said both Daltons were perfectly healthy, no reason they couldn't conceive. Just told me to tell them to keep trying."

My mouth goes dry. "Go on?"

"That didn't sit right with me," Chloe admits. "Addie seemed so genuine, and her husband—he gave me the creeps. I waited until the rest of the staff went to lunch—it was someone's birthday, Eliza's, I think—and snuck into Dr. Ellison's office to check her paper files."

"Paper files?"

"Dr. Ellison was old-school. She kept hard copies of everything in locked file cabinets. She didn't hide the key well, though. I found it in the top drawer of her desk." She chuckles. "Anyway, when I checked Addie's file, I found a lab report showing her husband was infertile. Zero sperm count. The lab didn't list a cause, but I've seen it before—sometimes it's genetic, sometimes developmental."

"Did you ask Dr. Ellison about it?"

"No way. She would fire me for snooping in her private files. I told Addie, though. She had a right to know."

My pulse kicks up. "How did you communicate with her?"

"She called again the next morning. I told her what I'd found. She asked for a copy of the report, so I mailed it—no email, no trace. I told her not to tell anyone where she got it." Chloe's voice trembles now. "And that's the last time I heard from Addie Dalton. Until yesterday, when you came to the office."

"Do you know if Clay has seen the report?" I ask.

"I'm sorry, I don't."

"Are these paper files still in Ellison's office?"

Chloe hesitates. "No, ma'am. They were stolen the night she was killed. Every cabinet emptied."

Amanda told me Ellison's database had been wiped clean. So why didn't she mention the paper files missing?

I picture the scene—Ellison's staff and half the Richmond PD stomping through the office, contaminating evidence, smudging fingerprints. I would've handled it differently. *Good job, Milo.*

Now I know with absolute certainty—I've stumbled onto something much larger than Addie's death.

Chapter Twenty-Seven

I arrive in Boone's office breathless and sweating and still reeling from what I've just learned.

From behind his desk, Boone gives me the once-over. "What the hell are you wearing, Sutherlin?" His voice is a low bark. "You on your way to a cocktail party?"

Heat scorches up my neck as I tug at the hem of the slinky dress. "It's not what it looks like."

His scowl deepens. "Then what is it? Start talking."

The photo of Clay's report burns in my palm like a live coal. There's so much I could tell him—but not yet. "Just tracking down a lead, sir. Nothing to talk about yet." I plop into a chair. "What's with the urgent message?"

Boone leans back, eyes narrowing as if he can smell my lie. "I just got a call from ME. The paternity test results are in—Clay isn't the father. I assume Ben is, but we'll have to test him to confirm."

I keep my face neutral even though my brain is sprinting. I hadn't considered what all this would mean for Ben. This paternity test paints a target square on his back. Every gossipy mouth in Tidewell will say he killed Addie because she wouldn't leave

Clay. But that's not Ben. He's kind and gentle. He would never kill the woman he loves, let alone his own child.

"Yoo-hoo, Lane?" Boone waves a hand. "You're a million miles away. Did you hear me? Ben's the father of Addie's baby."

"I heard." My face remains impassive, but inside I'm turning possibilities over like a chess move. This infertility report doesn't just clear Ben—it gives me leverage. If I hand it to Boone now, it becomes official, and everything goes into procedure: Clay gets warned, the case goes public. If I keep it, I control the timing. I can drop it like a bomb when Clay least expects it.

"Has Clay been notified of the results?" I ask.

Does Clay even know he's infertile? Makes sense that he does, that he killed Addie to prevent her from having another man's baby. But for now, I assume nothing. Too many loose ends. Too many questions.

Boone shakes his head. "Not yet. But I can't sit on something this important. I'll have to tell both Ben and Clay today."

I wet my lips, keeping my tone even. "Is Ben talking?"

Boone exhales hard through his nose. "Not yet. But he's lawyered up. He can't remain silent forever."

———

Thirty minutes later, at Slip 99, I catch snippets of chatter as I weave my way to the bar. The names on everyone's lips are *Ben* and *Clay*.

Cooter takes one look at me, pours a tequila shot, and slides it across the counter. "Rough morning?"

I think about my day so far—Dad's disappearing act, Wylie's ambush, the bombshell about Clay's infertility, and Dr. Ellison's cover-up. "You could say that." I jerk a thumb over my shoulder at the room. "What's going on with them? Sounds like March Madness—Team Ben versus Team Clay."

Cooter aims a finger gun at me. "Bingo. It hasn't let up since

Ben's arrest. I told you—Addie's murder lit the fuse. Ben's arrest is the explosion we all saw coming."

"Great!" I mutter. "What have I gotten myself into?" I toss back the tequila, embracing the burn.

Out of the corner of my eye, I spot Briggs striding through the doorway. He draws looks the way a current pulls the tide—effortless, natural, impossible to ignore.

He spots me and makes his way over.

"Are you following me?" I ask, brow arched.

"Hardly. I've been here nine months now. I'm a regular—you're the newcomer." He drops onto the stool beside me. "But someone *is* following you."

I glance around the restaurant, my gaze landing on Wylie at the far end of the bar. I spot Wylie at the far end of the bar and give him a sugary little wave—though we both know which finger I'd rather raise.

An argument erupts at a nearby table, and I crane my neck for a better look at the group of older women.

"I'm telling you, Clay wouldn't hurt a fly," one insists. "He worshiped the ground Addie walked on."

"Yeah?" another shoots back. "Then how come she was stepping out with Ben? You think she got pregnant by immaculate conception?"

A ripple of nervous laughter follows—half the table nodding one way, half the other.

I roll my eyes and turn back to Briggs. "Apparently, the town's gone tribal. Which are you—Team Ben or Team Clay?"

"I'm Team Justice, Lane." Cooter sets a black coffee in front of him, and Briggs takes a slow sip before continuing. "My sources say most of the women are rallying behind Clay—the golden boy, perfect husband. Most of the men think Ben's innocent. Either way, Tidewell's turned this into a popularity contest instead of a murder investigation."

I snort. "Or a civil war. Justice doesn't stand a chance in this circus—not when the judge is crooked and the victim's husband runs the town."

Briggs doesn't take the bait. Instead, he shifts gears. "Where'd you disappear to, anyway? Last time we talked, you promised me updates about Ben's boat. That was two days ago."

I swirl the empty shot glass between my palms, wishing for another. But I won't let Wylie and Clay be the reason I break my one-limit vow.

"Sorry. I've been a little busy keeping my father out of handcuffs and dodging trucks trying to run me off bridges."

Briggs's blue eyes widen. "Seriously? Who tried to run you off the bridge?"

I nod toward Wylie. "Two guesses. First one doesn't count."

Briggs follows my gaze, his jaw tightening. "And now he's following you. What's going on, Lane? You may think you can handle this alone, but you don't know what you're up against."

"I can take care of myself." I drop my eyes to the menu, pretending to study it even though the thought of food makes me nauseous.

I feel Briggs staring at me. "Something's bothering you. You gonna tell me what it is?"

I force a smile that doesn't stick. "You don't want what's rattling around in my brain."

"Try me." He leans in, voice low. "You've got instincts. I've got the law. If we're gonna keep the wrong man from going down, we'd better start working together."

I weigh his words, and more importantly, whether I can trust him. The answer comes clear and solid. Lawson Briggs was Tommy's life-long best friend. Tommy, who believed in justice, in doing right no matter the cost. Tommy, who was destined to follow in our father's footsteps to the bench. And Briggs? He's cut from the same cloth.

I glance over at Wylie. If looks could kill, I'd be deader than a doornail. "We can't talk here. Not with the Swamp King watching us. Meet me later—somewhere private?"

"Unfortunately, there's no *private* in your future. I know how he operates. Once he's on you, he's like marsh mud—sticks no matter how hard you scrub." He drums his fingers on the counter, thinking. "What say we walk out together now? That'll get under his skin. Dangerous move, but I'm game."

"Dangerous for you. He's already put a target on my back. Why would you step into my line of fire?"

Briggs tosses up his hands. "Someone's gotta save this town."

I nod toward the menu. "What about lunch?"

He drops a ten on the bar. "Forget lunch. I need fresh air. Let's walk the docks."

"Works for me," I say, sliding off the stool and following him out.

Outside, a cold front has settled over Oyster Bay. As we stroll the docks, the wind bites through my jacket and clears my head. I don't look back, but I can feel the Swamp King's stare dogging us until the bait shop blocks his view.

At the far end of a finger dock, Briggs drops onto the sun-warmed planks, long legs stretched out in front of him. I sit beside him, knees hugged to my chest, scanning the water as if answers might float up with the rising tide.

"Got a call from Boone on the way over," Briggs says. "Paternity test is back—Ben's the baby daddy."

"Yep. I heard. But I already knew. Are you ready for Tidewell's best-kept secret? Clay Dalton's infertile."

Briggs's head snaps toward me. "You're serious?"

"As a body bag."

I lay it all out—the trip to Richmond, Dr. Ellison's death, my conversation with Chloe Morgan. Then I show him the image of the fertility report on my phone.

Briggs's jaw tightens, the lawyer in him already calculating angles. "Infertile—and his wife shows up pregnant with another man's baby. Jesus, Lane. Clay had every reason to snap. And Ellison turning up dead? Makes you wonder what else is in those missing files?"

"Exactly. I'm *persona non grata* at Richmond PD; otherwise, I'd reach out to my contacts there. And I may still, if I get desperate." I drop my legs from my chest and straighten, drawing in a deep breath. "Clay and Addie sought treatment from Dr. Ellison. Clay ends up infertile, and Dr. Ellison covers for him. But why? Did they somehow know each other? What business would a small-town deputy have with a fertility specialist? It's too much of a long shot for the cases to be connected. Still, I can't let it go, can't shake the feeling I'm missing something."

"Remember, Lane. It's not just Clay. Whatever he's involved in, Wylie's in it too. And that opens up a whole new world of possibilities."

"I can't help but wonder if Addie somehow got caught up in it."

Briggs tilts his head. "A distinct possibility. It certainly would answer a lot of questions."

My pulse drums in my ears. "I'm not sure where we go from here. There's only one person alive who might shed some light on the situation—Ben." I lean forward, lowering my voice. "We need to get him to talk. He didn't kill Addie. He would never kill his own child. That's not who he is."

Briggs studies me for a long moment. "I believe you. And if we can get him talking—really talking—we might finally start peeling this mess back to the bone." He leans closer, voice dropping. "Be careful, Lane. Clay's not just covering his tracks anymore. He's hunting. And Wylie's holding his shotgun."

His warning hangs between us, heavy as an anchor. I drag in a breath, eyes on the dark water rippling beneath the docks. "You realize how deep we're in this now, right? We're not just solving Addie's murder. We're taking on the corruption that runs this whole town. Once we take this step, there's no going back." I turn to him, holding his gaze. "Are you ready for that, Briggs? Because you can still walk away."

Briggs looks away, staring out over Oyster Bay, silent long enough for me to think he might. But then his voice comes low. "I had no idea what I was walking into when I came back to Tidewell. The decay runs so deep here, half the time I can't tell what's real and what's not. You don't know how close I've been to packing up and leaving—maybe to Richmond, anywhere but here." He shifts, turning to face me fully. "But if you and I work together, maybe we stand a chance at saving this town before it eats itself alive."

I watch him, his words sinking deeper than I want to admit. Part of me wonders the same thing—what if I walk away? Pack up Dad and drive until Tidewell is a speck in the rearview mirror? Life would be simpler. Safer. But Dad already doesn't know where he is half the time. Tidewell . . . River Birch . . . is his home, the last place that still makes sense to him. And I won't be the one to take it away.

"I've second-guessed coming back a hundred times," I say quietly. "But every road out of here circles me back. Addie's gone. My father's slipping. This town is rotting from the inside out. If we don't fight for it, who will?"

Chapter Twenty-Eight

J udd calls on my way back to the sheriff's office. "Meet me at the farm as soon as possible."

Fear creeps up my spine. "Why? What's wrong? Is Dad okay?"

"He's fine. At least for now. No thanks to you." Then he hangs up.

I cut a sharp U-turn and head south on Tidewater Drive. Judd's pickup is already in the driveway, and I find him inside, pacing the living room while Dad watches his every step, hands working the hem of his shirt.

Judd spins when I come in, finger pointed at my chest. "You've really done it this time, Lane. There's a hit out on you. Now, everyone around you is at risk. Especially Dad, since you're living in his house."

I manage to keep a straight face. I can't let him see my fear. "Give me a break, Judd. Stop being so dramatic. Sure, some people in this town are corrupt, but they aren't the Mafia."

Judd goes perfectly still. "They're worse than the Mafia, Lane." His dark eyes bore into me. "You really have no idea, do you? Which makes you not just a lousy detective but dangerous."

"Who told you this, Judd?"

"A deputy friend of mine. One of the few good guys around here." His expression morphs from anger to anguish. "You need to leave town, Lane. I don't care where you go. Just get out while you can. I don't have room for Dad at my house, but I'll figure something out. Maybe Brandy and I will move in here."

Lally sweeps in from the kitchen with the telltale look of someone who's been listening from the next room. "The judge can stay with me. He'll be perfectly safe at Captain's Row."

I snap my head toward her, my face softening. "Thanks, Lally. But we're not dragging you into our mess."

"This isn't *our* mess, Lane." Judd's finger jabs inches from my nose. "This is *your* mess. Everything was fine until you cruised back into town."

Fury pulses through me, hot and unrelenting. "So fine that my best friend wound up murdered. So fine that the town now has its own brand of mafia?" My voice rises. "Don't you dare pin this on me, Judd. I'm just doing my job."

"Meanwhile, putting everyone in danger," Judd snarls.

"Quiet!" Dad's voice booms like he's back on the bench, settling his courtroom. "No one's going anywhere. I'm not a child. I don't need protecting."

"Maybe not, Dad, but you . . . but you . . ." Judd stutters, his words teetering on the edge of something I won't let him say.

I cut him a sharp look, willing him to shut up.

His jaw tightens, frustration sparking in his eyes. "I'm just saying, you haven't been yourself lately, Dad. And we're worried about you."

"Lane is the one we need to worry about." Dad's gaze falls on me, and for a moment, the years slip away. He's the judge again, and we're discussing one of his many cases. "Are you making progress in finding Addie's killer?"

"Yes, sir. We're on the verge of making a break," I say with more conviction than I feel. Something's coming. I can sense it. I just don't know if it's a breakthrough. Or a collapse.

"Then you must continue." He gestures toward his gun cabinet. "And don't you worry about a thing. I can protect myself."

Judd exhales, shoulders sagging, but the fight doesn't leave his eyes. "You're not making this easy, Dad." He pauses, thinking it through. "All right, you win—it's two against one. But I won't abandon you, not with everything going on. Maybe Brandy and I will move into the cottage, just for a bit, until things settle down. That way, someone's close if you need anything. It'll take some pressure off Lane."

I soften, smiling at my brother. "That would be great. Thanks, Judd."

"I'm doing it for him, not you," he grumbles.

My phone vibrates—a text from a number I don't recognize.

> Lane, Evan McCray here. Ben's ready to talk.
> He's requested an exclusive with you.

I fire back.

> On the way.

I wave the phone. "I've gotta go. Duty calls."

"I'll walk you out," Judd says, stepping in line beside me.

At the Bronco, he presses a folded slip of paper in my palm. "Here. Put this in your pocket. Fast. We're probably being watched. As soon as you get in the car, add that number to your phone. He's the deputy I told you about. The *only* one in the department you can trust."

"What about Boone?" I ask, sliding the paper into my pocket.

"Nope. Especially not him. He plays both sides to cover his own ass."

"Got it." I kiss his cheek. "Thanks, bro. And thanks for covering for me."

Steering one-handed down the driveway, I thumb Deputy Brody

Talcott's number into my phone. At the end of the drive, an old Chevrolet sits angled off the shoulder, its chrome dull in the afternoon haze. I'm not surprised when it eases onto the road behind me, keeping just far enough back to pretend it isn't tailing me.

I'm turning onto Main Street when Mama Jean's name lights up my screen. "Hey there," I answer. "I've been meaning to come see you."

"Then come now. I've got something I need to show you."

I check the dash clock. "Can it wait an hour? I'm in the middle of something right now."

Her voice sharpens, that no-nonsense edge cutting through the line. "I'm sorry, Lane. But it's important."

"Okay. Be there in a few."

At the next stoplight, I send a quick text to McCray.

Delayed. Won't be long.

I hang a right at the next corner, then another, watching the rearview mirror. The Chevrolet still lingers two cars back. I take a hard left onto a side street, then double back through the waterfront lot and down an alley that spits me out behind the courthouse. By the time I hit Tidewater again, the Chevrolet is gone.

Only then do I exhale, the tension in my shoulders easing. I've lost my tail. For now.

I turn toward Mama Jean's.

She's waiting at the front door, arms crossed tight and face pinched with exhaustion. Dark circles rim her eyes, and gray roots stripe her hairline. She's aged ten years since I saw her last week —before Addie's body was discovered, back when there was still hope of finding her alive.

"I saw something in Addie's closet," she says in a hushed rush. "Scared the tarnation outta me."

"Show me."

Taking me by the arm, she leads me through the living room and down the bedroom hallway. "The bathtub faucet sprung a leak, and I was looking for the valve to turn off the water," she explains. "Addie didn't think I knew about her hidey hole, where she stashed all her contraband in high school."

I fight back a smile as the memory surfaces—Addie and me in high school, crouched in her closet, smothering our giggles as we hid bootlegged booze and cigarettes in the hollow behind the wall.

Nothing appears to have changed in Addie's room since the last time I was here—the night before her wedding. Trophies still line the shelves, the pink canopy bed still dominates the space, the matching bureau squats along the opposite wall. It's as if time stopped here when she married Clay.

Mama Jean opens the closet door, and I drop to my knees. In the far corner is a small square panel, painted the same shade of cream, easy to miss unless you know it's there. The kind of thing you'd expect in an old house—pipe access for the adjacent bathroom. My fingers find the edges, and with a tug, the panel pops free. A black void yawns behind it like a lion's mouth.

I crane my neck to look up at Mama Jean. "Did you actually see what's in here?"

She bobs her head, eyes wide. "Scared me so bad, I shoved it right back in."

Dread slides cold through my gut as I reach into the cavity. My hand brushes against something soft and clammy. I nearly snatch my hand out, then I remind myself I'm a detective. I'm not allowed to be afraid. Inhaling a steadying breath, I drag out an old baby doll—pink dress faded, one arm askew, plastic dull from age and handling.

"She used to carry it everywhere," Mama Jean whispers. "She even slept with it till she was ten. When I saw it in there . . ." Her voice trails off, a shiver passing through her. "Something about it doesn't feel right. Why did she hide it—here, of all places?"

I don't state the obvious—she didn't want Clay to find it.

I brush the doll's stiff curls off her face. She looks a bit like Addie. "I agree. This is strange."

I examine the doll carefully, discovering the fabric back has been slit and re-stitched by hand. I slice open the seam with my pocketknife. When I shake the doll, a small flash drive slides into my palm. Then another. And another. Modern secrets sealed inside a child's toy. Whatever Addie found, it must be dangerous for her to bury it so deep.

Mama Jean gasps. "Lord, have mercy," she whispers. "Addie baby . . . what did you get yourself into?"

Slipping the drives in my jacket pocket, I stuff the doll back into the hole and snap the panel flush. I stand to face Mama Jean.

"Whatever this was might've gotten her killed," I say quietly. "You need to act like you never saw it. Don't tell anyone, don't mention the doll, forget you called me. I know it's hard, but your safety depends on it."

She clamps her hand over her mouth, the color draining from her face. "I—" she starts, then nods, too afraid to go on.

I squeeze her shoulder. "Don't worry, Mama Jean. I'll find out what happened to her. I'll make sure Addie didn't die in vain."

She swallows and forces a small, shaky smile. "God bless you, Laney."

I cast a nervous glance toward the door, hesitant to leave her alone. "I'm sorry, but I have to go. I'll call you later."

"Go." She kisses her fingertips and presses them to my lips. "Be safe, darling girl."

I hurry out of the room without looking back. The house exhales behind me. Outside, the air hits like a slap, cold settling into my bones.

I jump in the Bronco, the thumb drives burning a hole in my pocket. Whatever is on them will have to wait.

Chapter Twenty-Nine

The black Chevrolet is waiting down the street when I leave Mama Jean's, my personal escort to the sheriff's office. It doesn't follow me into the lot, just idles at the curb like a shadow that knows its place.

Inside, the station buzzes at low volume, deputies moving paper and coffee like it's any other day.

A baby-faced deputy with sandy hair and deep blue eyes steps out from behind the front desk. "Afternoon, Detective Sutherlin. Ben is waiting with his attorney in the interview room. I'll show you the way."

I glance down at his name tag—Deputy Brody Talcott, the name Judd scribbled on the slip of paper. One of the good guys. I know the way, and I don't need an escort, but his presence calms me.

As I fall in step beside him, he lowers his voice. "Judd gave me your number. He's a friend."

I nod curtly. "He told me."

"Don't hesitate to call if you need me."

"Back at you." I let a smile play at my lips, just in case anyone's watching.

The interview room smells of burnt coffee and floor wax, the overhead lights humming too loud.

Evan is at the table, sleeves rolled to his elbows, legal pad open. Ben sits hunched across from him, wrists cuffed, orange jumpsuit sagging off him like borrowed clothes. He doesn't lift his head when I walk in.

"Thanks for coming, Lane," Evan says, polite but clipped, like we're all on borrowed time.

When Ben finally looks up, fear flickers in his eyes. "Hey, Lane. Better roll tape. Might be the only testimony you get from me."

Dread settles cold in my chest as I lower myself to the chair beside Evan. "Why? What's going on?"

"Ben's receiving threats," Evan answers. "We're worried for his safety."

"Have you told Boone about this?"

Evan nods. "He promised to look into it, but he didn't seem too concerned."

"Thanks for telling me. I'll do what I can."

I stare across the table at my old friend—his tortured face, the swollen eyes. For a moment, the years fall away, and we're back in the high school cafeteria. Ben and Addie had been fighting, and I was talking him down, telling him how to make it right. How has it come to this? We've both lost our best friend. But Ben has lost something so much more—the love of his life.

I set my phone on the table and press the red circle on the voice recorder app. "Let's start at the beginning."

With a heavy sigh, Ben leans back, cuffed hands limp in his lap. "About nine months ago, Addie showed up on my doorstep out of the blue. She and Clay were having problems, and she needed advice."

"Why'd she come to you instead of Trina?" I ask.

"She wanted more than someone to listen. She wanted what we'd lost." A tear slips down his cheek. "We talked for hours that night. And then we slept together." His chin drops to his chest.

"Sleeping with a married woman goes against everything I believe in. But I couldn't help myself. It was Addie. *My* Addie. She was never supposed to be with Clay. She was supposed to be with me. He took her away from me. And I took her back."

I don't correct him, even though he and Addie had broken up long before she ever dated Clay.

I give him a moment. "Go on."

"She was miserable with Clay. He was controlling, manipulative."

"Was he ever abusive?"

"No. But she underestimated him. She was convinced he'd never hurt her." He sniffles, then looks up. "Clay's got his hands in the wrong cookie jar. Addie found out about some of his *so-called* business dealings." He lifts his cuffed hands, miming air quotes. "She refused to tell me the details—said I was safer if I didn't know. I warned her she was playing with fire, but she wouldn't stop."

Could those business dealings have anything to do with the thumb drives in my pocket?

Evan taps his pen against his legal pad, keeping tempo like this is a rehearsal. I want to snatch it from him, but I settle for a glare.

Ben wipes his nose on the sleeve of his jumpsuit. "She told me she was on the pill, but when she found out she was pregnant, she admitted she'd lied. She wanted a baby—was desperate for one. She hated having sex with Clay, but he was her husband, and she couldn't deny him without arousing suspicion."

Ben looks away, his pain twisted in something close to agony. "Then she found out Clay can't have children. His sperm don't swim. Somehow, he'd kept the results of his fertility test from her. She was livid—felt so betrayed."

I shake my head. "I can't imagine."

"Addie finally worked up the nerve to tell Clay about us. She told him she was pregnant and confronted him about his infertility. He threatened her—pressured her into raising the baby as their own." Ben's voice cracks, the words unraveling. "The night she died . . ." He chokes on the rest, tears leaving tracks down his face.

My heart aches for him. Love like that is rare—quiet, stubborn, the kind that endures. Whatever else Addie was hiding, she trusted him with the truth that mattered most.

I slide a wad of tissues toward him. "Take your time, Ben."

He grabs one, presses it against his eyes. When he looks up again, there's a faraway look on his face—he's reliving that night. He begins to sob, his words tumbling out too loud and too fast, as if he can outrun them. "She asked him for a divorce. He refused, and they had a terrible fight. He told her he'd kill her if she tried to leave him." His voice rises. "And he did. Clay killed her. Not me."

I reach forward, my hand hovering near his cuffed one. "Slow down, Ben. Breathe. We're not going anywhere. When you're ready, I need you to walk me through that night—step by step. Tell me exactly what happened."

Ben nods, forcing the breaths in and out. "She came to see me after their fight. She was such a mess." Another sob catches in his throat. "I tried to calm her down. I told her we'd take Scout and leave town—just the three of us. We'd have our baby somewhere so far away Clay could never touch us." He swipes at his face. "I had to pee. I told her not to go anywhere, but when I came back, she was gone."

"You went after her?"

"I tried. She had a head start on me—just disappeared into the night. I thought about going after her in my truck, but . . ." He shakes his head. "I figured she needed time to cool off. I called and called. It just rang and rang. No answer."

"We haven't been able to locate her phone yet."

"I'm sure it's at the bottom of some body of water." He stares at his hands. "I underestimated Clay. I never thought he would hurt Addie. Not Addie."

I lean forward. "Maybe he felt he had no choice. Is it possible he killed her because of what she knew about his business dealings?"

He lifts his swollen eyes to mine, voice ragged. "Yes! He was furious about the baby—that she got from someone else what he couldn't give her. But it was more than that. It was the secrets. Those damned secrets. Addie knew too much." His voice drops to a whisper. "That's why she's dead."

A chill works its way through me. What if it wasn't just Clay? What if someone else was in on it? What if Wylie ordered the hit?

A long silence stretches between us. When he speaks again, his voice is a whisper. "I don't care what happens to me, Lane. My life is nothing without Addie. This jail is crawling with Clay's men. They're threatening me. It's only a matter of time before they act. But I wanted you to know the truth in case something happens to me. I don't want to be remembered as a murderer. I want to be remembered as the man Addie loved most."

The words land like stones, and I feel each one. For a second I want to gather him up the way I did the night of the fight in high school—the night he bloodied his knuckles behind the gym because some jerk made a crack about Addie and she cried in the girls' bathroom. I dragged him home before the principal could call his daddy, and Addie patched him up with her first aid kit, like it was the most romantic thing in the world.

"Ben." I force my voice soft. "For the record, just in case there was any doubt in your mind, the paternity test proves you were the father." I don't know if I'm throwing gasoline on the fire, but he has a right to know.

He nods, chin quivering, unable to speak.

"I'll get you protection. We'll get you moved, whatever it takes. You won't be left sitting here."

He shakes his head, a tiny, hopeless movement. "Don't bother, Lane. It won't change what happened. My life's finished. They'll come for me no matter where I am."

The defeat in him is a thing I've seen before—nameless and heavy and old. I stand because I can't sit and listen to him give himself away. I go to his side of the table and fold my arms around him, awkward and careful, like he's broken and I don't want him to crumble. He leans into me with a surrendering kind of grief, and for a beat, he's the old Ben—not a suspect, not a headline, not a case file. He smells like the river and old cologne and regret.

"I won't let them hurt you, Ben," I say, meaning it with my whole body. "One day, when you're ready, you'll start over. And I'll be here for you every step of the way."

Evan clears his throat. From behind the plexiglass, I can feel eyes on me, watchful and hostile. Outside, the black Chevy still idles at the curb. Inside, I make a decision I can't say out loud yet. I'll pull every seam in this town until all the lies unravel.

Chapter Thirty

I call Boone as I'm leaving the interrogation room—one ring, straight to voicemail. I send him a text.

> Ben is being threatened. Get him protection.

I exit the double doors into the bright sunshine. Idling down the street to my right is the black Chevy, its engine humming like a warning.

I head off in the opposite direction, my finger on Briggs's number.

"I'm craving ice cream," I say when he picks up. "Grab your laptop and meet me at Dockside Creamery." A crowded spot, patio tables spilling onto the boardwalk, too many exit points for anyone to box me in.

With Ben's life hanging in the balance, I drive as fast as I dare toward the waterfront. I don't bother trying to shake the Chevy. He'll only find me again.

I order two scoops of salted caramel on a sugar cone and sit at a table on the edge of the seating area to wait. My eyes dart about —from the man in dark clothes to the guy on the flybridge of a nearby sportfisher, to the woman walking her dog along the dock. I sense them all watching, waiting for a chance to take me out.

By the time Briggs arrives, the ice cream is a melted mess in my hand, and my nerves are sizzling like an egg on hot asphalt in a Southern summer. I thrust the cone at him. "We can't talk here."

He takes a bite, then tosses the cone in a nearby trashcan.

I take off, striding down the boardwalk.

"Where are we going?" he asks, hurrying after me, laptop tucked under his arm.

I slow my pace. "Somewhere no one can hear us." I sweep an arm at the crowded waterfront. "Anyone could be listening."

He strokes his chin, thinking. "My sailboat's docked at Patriots Landing."

I shake my head. "Too risky. No exit."

He holds up his key fob. "We can go for a ride in my car."

I shake my head. "Might be bugged."

"Let's just walk the docks." He starts off.

I grab his arm, holding him back. "Stop, Briggs! I'm being watched. We could be in crosshairs as we speak."

"Geez, Lane. You're wound tight. You must have something good."

I finger the thumb drives in my pocket. "I'm not sure what it is, honestly. But based on my interview with Ben just now, it's the kind of dangerous that gets people killed."

My eyes sweep the crowd again, every face a potential threat. "I have an idea. Follow me." I burst through the door of Drift— the local late-night hangout.

The bartender looks up from stacking glasses. "Hey! What're you doing? We don't open for another hour."

I hold up my badge. "I need to borrow your rooftop."

He narrows his eyes. "I don't want any trouble. No shootouts."

I hold up a hand. "No shootouts. I promise. We're searching for someone. The vantage from your rooftop might help us find him."

He fishes keys from his pocket. "Okay. You can use it, but only for a few minutes. I don't want you scaring off my customers."

We climb the narrow wooden steps in single file to the top. Turning the key in the lock, he holds the door open for us. "It's all yours."

At the railing, the town spreads out below us—from Roxie's place in Oyster Bay Estates to Lally's in Captain's Row. String lights wink across the boardwalk, and a warm salt breeze off the river drifts around us.

Briggs nudges my arm. "Don't you own a computer?"

"I left it at home. I rarely need it. Mostly, I just use my phone." I open my hand, revealing the three thumb drives. "Mama Jean found Addie's old doll hidden in her closet. She got spooked and called me. Addie had sewn these inside the doll."

Briggs blinks hard, as though not believing what he's seeing. "People don't go to so much trouble unless they're scared." He gestures to a nearby table. "Shall we?"

We sit close so we can both see the screen. Briggs plugs in a drive, and a directory of Excel spreadsheets pops up. He clicks the first one. A list of patient names and dates fills the screen.

"Looks like a patient log," I murmur. "Names and appointment dates."

He leans closer, tracing a finger along the header. "Check this out. *Eggs harvested. Eggs frozen. Eggs transferred.*"

Our eyes meet. "Transferred where?" I ask, a sick weight settling in my gut.

Briggs swipes right. "What's this column?"

"Looks like numbers," I say. "Too short for Socials. Not birthdates either." I point at another tab at the bottom. "Try that one."

He clicks. A new sheet appears—rows of similar numbers, followed by dates, patient names, and eye-watering sums of money.

Silence stretches between us, broken only by the soft hum of the laptop fan.

I press my fingers to my lips. "You don't think . . ." The thought is too awful to finish.

Briggs nods, exhaling slowly. "I think they are trafficking harvested eggs—human embryos."

My stomach turns. "What the hell? That sounds like something out of a conspiracy thread. You ever heard of anything like this?"

"Unfortunately," Briggs says, eyes still fixed on the screen. "It's called ova trafficking—harvested human eggs sold on the black market, usually to wealthy couples overseas where regulations are loose or nonexistent."

I shake my head, still in disbelief. "That's awful, but it makes sense. So many young women are harvesting eggs these days—it's become almost routine. You sign a few forms, trust the doctors to handle the science, and the eggs are waiting for you when you're ready to start a family." I point at a line item with a seven-figure payout. "For that kind of money, they can have all my eggs."

He huffs out a dry laugh. "Right—and twenty years later, when you see your own face on every stranger in town, you'll only have yourself to blame."

I shoot to my feet and start pacing between the railing and the chair. "They murdered Ellison and grabbed the files—basically dismantled the whole operation. Did the doctor do something to piss them off? Was she threatening to turn them in or stop delivering eggs?"

Briggs looks up at me. "She's dead. Whatever the reason, they took care of it."

I chew a hangnail. "I should turn this over to Richmond PD. It's evidence in their murder investigation."

"You should. But you can't. Not yet. Not if we're going after Clay and Wylie. Besides, it's evidence in *our* murder investigation too."

Briggs copies the folders to his laptop, ejects the drive, and then does the same with the other two. He stands and presses the drives into my palm. "We comb this for any names, payments, appointment overlaps—anything that touches Clay or Wylie."

"Right. But I doubt we'll find anything. Addie's death is the only thing we have tying them to this. And it's circumstantial. I have a hunch others, like Tate, are involved. Clay and Wylie aren't smart enough to pull this off alone."

Briggs drops into his chair with a groan. "If I could rewind to this afternoon, I'd have walked away when you gave me the chance."

"Too late now, Briggs. You're in it neck-deep." I unlock my phone, forward the audio file, and feel it whoosh off. "I interviewed Ben. I just sent you the recording. His statement could corroborate what's on these drives. But first, we have to keep him alive."

Briggs's head snaps up. "What do you mean, keep him alive?"

"He's being threatened. Boone said he'd look into it, but I'm not holding my breath. He's in even more danger now that word's out he's the baby daddy. Clay can't handle the public humiliation. We need to get Ben protection. Fast."

"How do you propose we do that?" he asks.

"Hire outside security. Move him to Richmond. I don't care how. We just can't leave him sitting like a target in that cell."

Briggs shakes his head. "Private guards aren't allowed in Tidewell's jail. They'd be useless once the door locks anyway. The only real option is a transfer—to another jurisdiction."

"Then file for one. Petition the court. Whatever it takes."

His mouth hardens. "Judge Tate would never approve it."

I meet his gaze. "Then we go around him. There are other judges in the district."

Briggs rubs his temples. "Let me sleep on it. If only we had a little more evidence—something that puts Clay closer to Addie that night."

Frustration knots in my chest. He's playing it safe. And Ben might die while he dithers. I start for the stairs, yelling to him over my shoulder. "Sure, Briggs. Get your beauty rest. Clay's counting on it."

I'm halfway down the stairs when my phone buzzes. "Detective Sutherlin? This is Joe at Patriots Landing. We pulled Camera 3, timeframe nine until midnight, from the night in question. Thought you'd want a look."

"Send it," I say, spelling out my email address.

Seconds later, my phone pings with the incoming email. I head for my Bronco, eyes fixed on the spinning wheel as the footage loads. By the time I slide into the driver's seat and lock the doors, the clip is playing.

My heart lurches, a sick tumble, when I see Addie and Scout—on her pink leash—leaving Ben's boat at 9:23. These are her final minutes, and I'm powerless to reach through the screen to save her. I hold my breath, praying I don't see Ben going after her. The screen stays mercifully empty—no action, just the stillness of a sleepy night at the marina.

Until five minutes later, when a dark pickup truck circles the marina parking lot. When the license plate comes into view, I freeze the frame and zoom in.

VA 212, the Northern Neck plate—pale blue background, a skipjack sailboat drifting on calm water, and the words The Northern Neck stamped along the bottom.

My pulse spikes. Everyone in Tidewell knows that number—it's been in the Dalton family for generations. Clay doesn't just drive that Dodge Ram, he parades it through town like a crown on wheels. And now it's caught on tape, less than a mile from where I found Scout. From where Addie disappeared.

I remember the message Addie left me the night of her murder. At 9:42 p.m. The rumble of an approaching engine in the background. "Bingo," I say to the screen. "I've got you now, Clay."

I screenshot the image and fire it off to Briggs:

Clay's truck in Patriots Landing parking lot around the time of Addie's murder. Is this that little more evidence you're looking for?

I'm backing out of the email when another message pops up from Joe: *The original's still on the system. You want me to pull it onto a drive?*

I respond right away. *Please. Don't delete anything. I'll come get it myself.*

Dropping my phone in the console, I start the engine and peel out of the parking lot. As I head toward the marina, my pulse steadies into something colder than fear, sharper than grief. Clay Dalton just slipped, and I've got the proof to prove it.

The pieces are finally locking into place—Addie's last steps, Scout on her pink leash, Clay's truck circling like a vulture. The leash is the biggest victory—proof that Clay planted it on Ben's boat. If Ben had killed her, he would've gotten rid of the murder weapon. A defense attorney will still try to spin it, but the tape won't lie. I'll watch it through, though my gut says it's blank.

Hold on, Ben, I think, gripping the wheel tighter. *This time, I'm not letting the truth disappear.*

Chapter Thirty-One

The aromas of garlic and onion greet me when I enter the house an hour later. I'm surprised to find Brandy and Judd at the stove instead of Dad, who's perched on a barstool, watching them with a contented smile.

Brandy stirs a pan of sizzling onions, the wooden spoon moving in steady circles, while Judd chops tomatoes too carefully, like he's afraid of nicking his fingers. Their laughter mingles with the crackle from the pan, a picture so normal it feels foreign after the day I've had.

Dad catches sight of me in the doorway. "Your brother finally learned the difference between a paring knife and a steak knife," he says, dry amusement in his voice.

"Barely," Judd says with a chuckle.

Brandy elbows him in the side. "We've been taking cooking lessons. Online, of course. It's the only thing we enjoy doing together."

"True that," Judd says. "She thinks fishing is gross, and I hate to shop."

She cuts him a look. "I do more than shop, thank you very much."

I remain in the doorway, letting myself breathe and soaking in the domestic calm. I picture their days—Judd at the boatyard, Brandy giving facials to wealthy clients—simple and steady compared to mine. A bittersweet smile tugs at my lips. I wish I were more a part of their lives. But even their obvious happiness doesn't loosen the knot in my chest.

I continue into the kitchen, reaching for the bottle of red on the counter. I have a long night ahead of me, and I'd planned to get straight to work, scrutinizing the thumb drives and video Joe sent from Patriots Landing. But I could use a break to clear my mind first. Why not enjoy a nice dinner with my family before diving back into the shadows?

"Tough day?" Dad asks, watching me fill the glass to the brim.

"Yes, sir. But we're making progress."

I notice Scout standing at the French doors, tail swishing, waiting to be let out. "What's wrong with y'all? Can't you see the poor dog needs to pee?"

Brandy looks over. "Oh. Oops. Sorry."

I follow the dog onto the patio, breathing in the brisk fall evening. The sun's setting earlier now, and the distant scent of wood smoke reminds me that winter isn't far off.

I startle when Dad says my name. I hadn't heard him come out. "What's bothering you, Bug?"

"Just this case. Is it possible to get a new judge assigned?"

Dad shakes his head slowly. "Possible. But not easy. You'd need to change venues. We don't have another judge in Tidewell." His eyes narrow. "Why? What's Tate done now?"

"Nothing yet." My voice dips low, heavy with the weight of it. "But Ben's being threatened, and I'm afraid for his life. We finally have enough evidence to get an arrest warrant for Clay, and I have a sick feeling Tate won't play ball. He'll find a way to bury it."

"If the evidence is strong enough, he can't bury it without rousing public suspicion."

"Hmm. I hadn't thought of that." I turn to face him, leaning against the railing and sipping my wine. "Did Tate have something to do with your early retirement?"

Dad grimaces. "You might say that."

"What'd he do?"

"He undermined me with the lawyers, told them I was slipping. He wanted my seat, and he wanted it clean—no scandal, just the quiet rumor that Hollis Sutherlin was losing his edge." Dad rubs his temple, his hand veiny and mottled with age spots. "I could've fought. Maybe I should've. But I couldn't argue with the truth. I *was* slipping. So I walked away."

"I get that he wanted your seat, but couldn't he have waited a few more years?"

Dad lifts a bony shoulder. "Tate despises anyone on the right side of justice. He uses his position to corrupt and control. He couldn't afford to wait, wanted me out of the way so he could run this town unchecked."

I can tell there's more to it, something heavier he's not saying. But I don't press. Instead, I set my glass on the railing and meet his weary eyes. "Then I'll do what you couldn't. I'll stand up to him."

His mouth tightens, pride and fear warring in the lines of his face. "Watch your back, Bug. You're not just taking on Tate."

I frown. "What do you mean?"

He exhales slowly, like the words have been lodged in his chest for years. "They call themselves the Old Guard. Families like the Daltons—men like Tate and Wylie—have been passing power down from father to son in this county since before you and I were born."

The name chills me—*Old Guard*—heavy with history and menace. Suddenly Clay's truck, Tate's smug smile, Wylie's threats—none of it feels isolated anymore. It's a machine. And I've just stepped into its gears.

Dad stares out toward the darkening creek, voice low. "Back in the day, they claimed to have the town's best interests at heart.

Maybe they even believed it. But that got lost somewhere along the way. Now they only care about themselves. And Bug . . ." His eyes flick to mine, sharp and sad all at once. "They'd tie a cement block to your foot and drop you overboard without thinking twice about it."

Chapter Thirty-Two

My vibrating phone jerks me out of a deep slumber on Friday morning. I fumble around on the nightstand until my hand lands on it. My vision's still blurry, and I have to blink hard to see Brody Talcott's name glowing on my screen. My stomach drops. A call this early can't be good.

It's six thirty, still dark outside. The days are getting shorter, sunrise lagging behind, but dread is already wide awake in my chest.

"Sutherlin," I mutter into the phone.

"Sorry for the early call, Detective. There's been an incident. Ben Holloway's been rushed to the hospital."

I scramble upright in bed, Scout springing to attention beside me, ears perked. "Where? What happened?"

"A guard found him unresponsive this morning. EMS started CPR and got him to Tidewell Regional. His pulse is faint. They're calling it an overdose."

"Preserve the cell," I say with a calm I don't feel. "Get me every camera feed from the jail and the booking area, every custody log, every officer who had access after midnight. Where's Boone?"

"On his way to the hospital."

"Good. I'll meet him there." I throw back the covers. "Stay on this, Deputy. Based on the threats Ben's been getting, we have to assume someone tried to make this look like a suicide."

"I'm on it," Brody says, his voice clear and alert.

The house blurs around me as I throw on clothes and run a toothbrush across my teeth. I'm grateful to find Judd at the stove, scrambling eggs.

He glances at me over his shoulder. "Morning. Want some eggs?"

I debate telling him about Ben but decide against it. When word gets out, I don't want it coming from the Sutherlin family. "Unfortunately, I don't have time. I just got an emergency call, and I have to go to town. Can you stay with Dad until Lally arrives at nine?"

"Sure." He pours coffee into a paper cup and presses it into my hand. "Here. Sounds like you're gonna need this."

"Thanks, bro." For a moment, it's like we're back in high school, fending for ourselves after Mom left us. When did we drift apart? Was it my fault? His? Or a little of both? But he's here now, making breakfast for Dad. He's trying. And so must I. Dad needs us both right now. And even if it costs me my job in Richmond, I'll be here for him. I won't let Judd bear this burden alone.

Scout pads at my heels as I head toward the mudroom. "Stay here, girl."

But she slips out the door behind me anyway. She senses something important is happening, and she wants to be a part of it.

I crank up the rock music on the way to the hospital, needing something stronger than caffeine to keep me upright. I was up half the night combing through the security footage and the thumb drives for anything useful to the case. But I came up empty on both counts.

The ER smells like disinfectant and burnt coffee. The desk nurse glances from Scout to me. "Dogs aren't allowed in the hospital."

"She's K-9," I say, flashing my badge. "I'm here about Ben Holloway."

She rolls her eyes. "You and everyone else. Take a seat. The doctor will be out soon."

I spot Boone in the far corner of the waiting room, head tilted back, eyes closed. When I plop down beside him, he startles, eyes suddenly wide.

"Sleeping at a time like this?" I ask in a sarcastic tone.

He ignores it. "This is a hospital, Sutherlin. Get that dog out of here."

"She stays. I brought her to protect Ben. He clearly needs a guard dog since you can't keep him safe."

Boone grunts and looks away.

"How'd this happen?" I ask.

He lifts his phone. "Just got a text. They found a packet of pills in his bunk. Appears to be a suicide attempt."

My skin goes cold. "A packet of pills? That's a tidy little story now, isn't it?"

Boone narrows his eyes. "What are you suggesting, Sutherlin? I'm not in the mood for mind games."

"Neither am I, Sheriff. Ben was receiving threats, and now he's fighting for his life. The packet of pills isn't a suggestion—it's a logical assumption. McCray warned you Ben was receiving threats. This happened under your watch, Sheriff."

Color creeps up Boone's neck. "I'm aware, Sutherlin. I questioned Ben yesterday evening. He couldn't give me any details?"

"You mean, he *wouldn't* give you any details. Why would he rat out the people who are threatening him? Did you put extra security on him?"

He shakes his head. "Didn't think it was necessary."

I hesitate but decide not to press it now. "We have enough evidence to arrest Clay."

Boone looks skeptical. "On what grounds?"

I tell him about my conversation with Ben and the marina

footage. "So tell me, Boone, are you ready to arrest Clay, or are you going to keep looking the other way?"

I hold my breath. This is the moment. Is he Team Clay, Team Ben, or Team Justice?

He shifts in his chair. "You may be *from* here, Sutherlin, but you don't *belong* here. You're playing a dangerous game. I can take that badge away from you as quickly as I gave it to you."

I pull the badge from my pocket and set it on the armrest. I lean in, lowering my voice so only he can hear. "Try it. But you'll have to explain to the commonwealth's attorney why you stripped the only detective in this department while a murderer walks free. And don't forget, Sheriff—you're an elected official. If the voters find out you're protecting the Old Guard, your next term ends before it starts."

His face goes red, steam practically rising off of him. "You're right, Sutherlin. Sheriffs are elected in this county. I don't answer to you *or* Briggs. I answer to the people. And the people don't want chaos. They want order. My order."

Our gazes lock on the badge. I snatch it up and shove it into my pocket. "Good. Then you won't stand in Briggs's way when he requests the arrest warrant."

He shakes his head, expression grim. "I'm sorry, Lane. My hands are tied."

I press my lips tight. "Fine. But you're making a mistake. I *will* arrest Addie's killer, Old Guard be damned."

He's about to say something when a young doctor appears from behind the double doors and calls, "Family of Ben Holloway?"

"Did you contact Ben's family?" I ask Boone as we cross the room.

"Not yet," he snaps in a guilty tone that tells me he forgot.

The doctor is younger than me, clean-cut with warm brown eyes. He offers a quick nod to Boone. "Sheriff."

He shifts his weight, the gravity in his expression clear. "We were able to stabilize Mr. Holloway, but he's not out of the woods yet. We pumped his stomach—nothing toxic there, which didn't add up. So we did a closer examination and found a puncture mark on his arm. Whatever knocked him out didn't come from pills. We're running the labs now."

Boone tenses beside me. I don't dare look at him.

"We found pills in his cell," I tell the doctor. "Is it safe to assume someone planted them to support the suicide narrative?"

Boone cuts his eyes at me. "Don't put the doc on the spot, Sutherlin. His job is to save lives, not solve crimes. We'll know more once the tox screen comes back."

I keep my focus on the doctor. "Can I see Ben? He's an old friend."

The doctor cast a sympathetic gaze at me. "I'm sorry. Family only right now. We've notified his parents. They're on the way. If you give me your contact information, I'll call you if anything changes."

I recite my name and number, and he fingers them into his tablet. "I need to get back to the patient. I'll be in touch soon," he says, and he heads back through the double doors.

I pivot on my heels and head for the exit.

"Where're you going, Sutherlin?" Boone calls after me.

"To see Briggs," I say without looking back.

He catches up and grips my arm hard. "Deputizing you was a mistake. You're out of your league, Sutherlin. Tate will never green-light Clay's arrest."

I stop dead, meeting his stare. "He might—if you stopped running cover for him. Give me your support, Sheriff. The town's eating itself alive, split over which man murdered Addie. We can end this right now by arresting the real killer."

His jaw works, but all he can manage is, "I can't."

I bark a humorless laugh. "Of course you can't. You've been Team Clay from the start. Just like you were Team Wiley nineteen years ago." I pin my glare on him, refusing to blink. "I was just a kid, and you turned your back on me. You told me to stay quiet, said my family had suffered enough. So I carried it all these years. No justice. No peace."

His response comes out thin. "I was trying to protect you."

"Protect me?" My voice cuts sharper than glass. "I've lived with the cost of that so-called protection every day since. You were supposed to stand up for me. Instead, you stood down."

His face crumples, a mix of shame and stubborn pride, but I'm already turning away. "Save it, Sheriff. You made your choice a long time ago."

I don't look back as I push through the sliding doors, Scout close at my side.

Chapter Thirty-Three

I call Briggs on my way to his office. When he picks up, I skip the pleasantries. "They hit Ben. Injected him with a lethal dose of sedatives. Planted a packet of pills in his cell to make it look like suicide. Brody found him in time. He's in the ER—sedated but stable." I grip the wheel tighter. "We're racing against the clock, Briggs. It's Friday. We need Clay in custody today, or this town goes up in flames by Monday."

Briggs exhales a heavy sigh. "I've been up since four drafting the affidavit for the warrant. I'll add the threat on Ben's life and walk it over to the courthouse."

"I'm coming with you. I'm almost at your office."

"Fine. I could use caffeine before we face Tate. Meet me at the Salty Bean. You can walk me through the details while I finish the draft, then we'll take it to him together."

"Perfect. See you in five."

I hold it together until I see Briggs in line at the coffee shop. He reminds me so much of Tommy it steals my breath, and suddenly everything crashes down—losing my best friend, almost losing Ben, realizing how far I've drifted from the people who matter most. Tears spill before I can stop them.

Scout presses against my leg, whimpering softly, as if she feels the storm breaking inside me.

"Hey." Briggs pulls me into his arms, rubbing my back. "What's wrong?"

I can't answer. The lump in my throat won't let the words through.

When the young woman behind the counter asks for our order, I push back from him. "God, I'm sorry. I don't know what got into me. Just . . . facing some old ghosts, I guess."

He smiles softly. "I get it. You've been through a lot. You can cry on my shoulder anytime."

I shake my head and snatch a napkin from the dispenser, dabbing at my eyes. "No more crying today. We need to focus on arresting Clay."

Briggs nods once. "Right. We've got our work cut out for us."

I grab a table while Briggs orders our coffees. When he joins me, I lay out everything I know about the attempt on Ben's life. We spend thirty minutes tightening the affidavit—cross-referencing timelines, checking witness statements, closing every loophole Tate could exploit.

We agree not to mention the thumb drives. Whatever Addie uncovered about the embryo trafficking is too volatile, and we have nothing tying Clay directly to it. For now, the cases will have to run in parallel. Besides, there's a good chance Tate's in on that scheme too.

"What happens if Tate denies the warrant?" I ask as we cross the square on the way to the courthouse.

He gives me a sidelong glance. "You mean, *when* he denies it?"

I elbow him in the side. "I was trying to be optimistic. But you're right—we need to be realistic." I drop my head, staring down at the sidewalk. "We need eyes on the case. I've got a couple of contacts at Richmond news outlets, but I doubt they'd care about Tidewell. Corruption's not headline material unless it bleeds."

"Don't worry. I'm one step ahead of you. My secret weapon's on standby."

I frown. "Your secret weapon? What's that?"

A mischievous smile tugs at his lips. "You mean *who*. You'll see soon enough. I have a feeling the two of you will hit it off beautifully."

Judge Tate keeps us cooling our heels outside his chambers for nearly an hour while he *reviews* the affidavit. When his assistant finally ushers us in, his first words are a bark. "Get that dog out of here. This is a courtroom, not a kennel."

"Sorry, Judge." I keep my voice even as my hand finds Scout's head. "She's Addie's dog. She hasn't left my side since the murder. She stays."

His eyes darken with irritation, but I don't flinch. Scout just settles at my feet, calm as ever, like she knows exactly what's at stake.

"Then get out of my office and take her with you." He tosses the affidavit across his desk at us like it's spoiled fruit. "Denied. All circumstantial. Nothing here justifies an arrest."

Briggs stiffens beside me. "Then what about a search warrant for Dalton's house and truck? The security footage and Holloway's testimony establish probable cause."

Tate's smile is thin, almost pleased. "Still circumstantial. I won't approve a fishing expedition. Bring me hard evidence, and we'll talk. Until then, this conversation is over."

Anger pulses through me. "Insufficient? We have Clay on tape the night of the murder, less than a mile from where I found her dog. And you've got Ben's testimony. They tried to kill him, for crying out loud. Won't you at least talk to the ER doctor?"

He wags a finger at me, his voice sharp as a whip. "Watch your tone, young lady. Remember who you're talking to. Come back when you have something concrete."

I storm out of Tate's chambers, Scout at my side, Briggs on my heels. I don't slow until we hit the courthouse steps. "I hope your secret weapon is everything you claim."

"I'm not worried," Briggs says, a faint smile tugging at his mouth. "Alex covered politics in DC for twenty years. She knows how to make people listen—especially the ones who don't want to."

Intrigued, I ask, "How'd she end up here?"

"She got sick of the DC corruption. She moved here with her husband, but they've since divorced. By then, she'd fallen in love with Tidewell and decided to stay."

"Is she a reporter or what?"

"She's the face of *Tidewell Unfiltered*."

My jaw drops. "As in the Facebook group half this county follows?"

"Bingo." He pulls out his phone, thumbs flying. "I'm texting her now, asking her to meet us in my office."

———

The blinds in Briggs's office are half-drawn, slicing the late-morning sun into hard lines across his desk. Scout noses the floor for crumbs while I pace, too keyed up to sit. The door swings open, and Alex Monroe walks in. Striking doesn't cover it—dark hair, darker eyes, a presence that fills the room before she even speaks.

When Briggs stoops to kiss her cheek, her hand lingers on his chest a second too long. Older than him—forties, maybe—but polished, magnetic. Either she's got a crush on him, or they're more than friends. The pang that stabs through me catches me off guard.

"So, boys and girls, whose cage are we rattling first?" Alex drops her bag on the chair like she owns the place.

"Only one cage today." Briggs flashes his brightest smile, but it fades as fast as it comes. "I'd offer you a seat, but time is of the essence. Ben Holloway is in the hospital, clinging to life. Someone injected him with a massive dose of sedatives and planted a packet of pills in his cell to make it look like suicide."

"Either Clay Dalton or one of his lackeys," I cut in.

Briggs nods. "Judge Tate just denied my request for an arrest warrant for Clay, even though we have what I believe to be ample evidence. Truth is, Alex, the less you know, the safer you are."

Alex's dark eyes flash. "Ooh. Now, I'm intrigued. I've been waiting for the opportunity to rat on Tate. During my divorce, the jerk sided with my ex's powerful family in a property dispute. I'll never forget the way he dismissed me in chambers, like I didn't matter."

Briggs's expression hardens. "Sounds exactly like Tate."

Alex twists her dark hair into a messy bun, eyes cold. "We'll go after him, and I promise you, we'll make him regret it. But he won't back down. Do you have another judge who'll actually do their job?"

"As a matter of fact, I do." He pulls out his phone and scrolls. "I have an appointment with Judge Carmichael in Miller's Crossing at three o'clock."

My eyes narrow. "Since when?"

"I emailed him while we were waiting for Alex. I didn't want to get your hopes up." He waves the phone, a small grin breaking through. "He just wrote back. He's more than happy to review the affidavit. From the sound of it, Carmichael isn't exactly Tate's biggest fan either."

I clap my hands. "All right. Let's get to it. How do you want to handle the publicity blitz, Alex?"

"I'm thinking Facebook Live from in front of the ER entrance. I hate to use poor Ben like this, but people eat up these human-interest stories."

My face falls. "Ben won't mind. He's not only fighting for his life; he's facing a potential life sentence. And we're in a position to help him."

Alex's expression softens. "You two are close, aren't you?"

My throat tightens. For someone who never cries, I've been doing a lot of it lately. "We used to be. Addie Dalton was my best friend. The baby she was carrying was Ben's."

"Oh, honey." Alex reaches for my hand, squeezing gently. "I'm so sorry. If you're up to it, I'd love to put you on the live feed."

I swallow hard, weighing the risk. "If you think it'll help . . ."

"It will," Alex says without hesitation. "People need to see your face, hear your conviction. That's what will cut through Tate's games."

"Then let's roll," I say, heading for the door.

Alex offers to drive, but with Scout in tow, I follow them in my Bronco. I trail close, watching their heads bob as they talk, animated and easy. That pang stabs me again. After Grayson cheated on me, I vowed myself to a life of celibacy. I didn't think I could ever have feelings for another man. Turns out my heart still works. I'm just not ready to risk it breaking all over again.

At the ER entrance, Alex whips a small tripod from her bag and clips her phone into place. "We'll keep it tight. Sixty seconds, maybe ninety. Long enough to light a fire; not long enough to bore them." She checks her reflection in the black screen, then points the phone at me. "You'll stand here. Scout at your side. Nothing softens a message like a loyal dog."

My stomach drops. "This is a bad idea."

"You'll do great," Alex says, calm but firm. "People need to see the face of someone who's fighting back."

She taps her phone, and the red light comes on. "Good morning, Tidewell," Alex begins, her voice smooth, practiced. "I'm Alex Monroe with *Tidewell Unfiltered*. I'm here at Tidewell Regional, where Ben Holloway is fighting for his life after what officials are calling an apparent suicide attempt. But not everyone believes that story."

She turns the camera to me.

The lens feels like a spotlight, hotter than any interrogation. Scout leans into my leg, steadying me. "My name is Detective Lane Sutherlin. Addie Dalton was my best friend. Ben Holloway —the father of her unborn child—is now in this hospital because someone wanted him silenced. We have evidence to arrest Addie's real killer. But Judge Vernon Tate is stonewalling us. We will not stop until the truth comes out. Tidewell deserves better. Ben deserves justice. And Addie deserves to be remembered. Let your voices be heard."

The camera lingers on me for a beat too long before the screen finally blinks dark.

I turn to Briggs. "Well?"

He exhales hard, shoulders sagging. "Great job, Lane. I just hope we know what we've started—because there's no going back now."

Chapter Thirty-Four

Alex's phone vibrates before we make it back to our cars.

"It's blowing up," she says, eyes twinkling. "You've just set this town on fire."

I punch the air. "Great! Now what?"

Briggs checks his watch. "It's almost noon. I'll need to leave around two to get to Miller's Crossing by three. Which means Tate has two hours to change his mind and issue the warrant. Lunch on me at Cricket's."

Alex clicks her doors unlocked. "Perfect. That'll give us a clear view of the courthouse."

On the drive back to the square, I get a call from an unidentified number. I answer it anyway. "Sutherlin."

"Detective, this is Dr. Greene, attending physician for Ben Holloway. He's awake and asking to see you."

Relief floods me. "That's excellent news, Doctor. I just left the hospital, and I'm tracking down some important leads. I know it's against protocol, but could you put him on for just a minute? Please."

Green hesitates. "Considering the circumstances, I can let it slide this once."

A shuffle of movement, then Ben's raspy voice cuts in. "I

didn't do this, Lane. I would never kill myself—no matter how bad things get. I was asleep in my cell, and I woke up to Clay jabbing a needle in my arm."

My blood runs cold. *Clay. In the cell himself. The arrogance.* "Are you sure it was Clay?"

"I'm positive." He breaks into a fit of coughing, then comes back hoarse. "A nurse told me what you did—the Facebook thing. Your support means a lot. Thanks."

"That's only the beginning, Ben. I've got your back. You just concentrate on getting better."

"I will. Do I have to go back to jail?"

"Not if I can help it. Now put the doctor back on for me."

Dr. Green's voice returns. "We'll need to keep him overnight for observation."

"Can you stretch that through the weekend? I want as few people as possible to know he's conscious. Whoever did this might try again."

"I can make that work. I'll divert questions from the press, limit staff access, and move him to ICU—visitor restrictions are tighter there. I'll bend the rules this once if it means keeping him safe."

"Perfect. We'll have a guard posted too. Thank you, Doctor. Please update me on any changes."

I pull into the parking lot behind Cricket's and slip the Bronco into park. I hit Brody's number. He answers on the first ring.

"Ben's awake," I blurt.

"I heard," Brody says, his tone upbeat. "Dr. Green called me a few minutes ago."

"Let's keep it quiet for now. The fewer people who know, the safer he is. He'll stay in the hospital through the weekend. Do you have deputies you trust to guard him?"

"A couple," he says. "We'll rotate shifts. Don't worry, Lane— we won't let anything else happen to him. Oh, and nice job with the Facebook Live. The town's cheering for you."

"Minus a few nefarious sorts," I mutter, ending the call.

Inside Cricket's, Briggs and Alex are already seated at a table by the window. He smiles when he sees me. "There you are. I thought we lost you. I ordered you a chicken salad croissant. I hope that's okay."

I force a smile. "Great, thanks." I love the house specialty, but my stomach's too knotted to even think about food.

I slide into the seat, debating whether to tell them about Ben. Alex sits back, composed—borderline smug. I trust Briggs. But I don't have a firm read on her yet. I'm not sure if she's in it to save Ben . . . or to even the score with Tate.

The waitress sets down a bowl of water, and Scout dives in, lapping noisily while the square outside hums with movement. I glance up and freeze. The sound isn't idle chatter. It's shouting. Chanting. A crowd gathering with picket signs, massing on the courthouse steps.

My eyes widen. "Whoa. Check that out."

Alex pumps a fist. "Yes! All we need now is an appearance by the Honorable Judge Vernon Tate." She shoots to her feet. "In fact, I'm going to camp out on those steps and wait for him."

"I'm coming too," I say, already rising.

Briggs chuckles. "Y'all go ahead. I'll have our waitress bag our order."

As we cross the square, the crowd swarms us with questions. Cameras flash, voices rise, and Scout presses close against my leg. I raise my hand, holding them off. "No further statement at the moment," I call out.

A few minutes later, Briggs strides up, paper sack in hand. "Just got off the phone with my source inside the courthouse. Their phones are blowing up."

"Excellent. Our plan is working." Alex holds her phone up, camera trained on the double doors. "Tate can't leave this court-house without making headlines."

We settle in to wait, picking at our croissants. An hour drags by before Tate finally appears, flanked by staff, his face pinched with irritation. He pauses on the top step, his black robe billowing in the breeze, and the crowd goes silent.

"Why's he wearing his robe?" I whisper to Briggs.

"To remind everyone who's in charge."

Tate lifts his chin, voice booming across the square. "I will not be blackmailed by your three-ring media circus. There is not enough evidence in the Addie Dalton murder case for a search warrant, let alone an arrest. My decision stands."

The courthouse doors slam behind him, but the crowd erupts in response. First a single voice, then a chorus, rising into a chant that echoes off the brick facades. "Save Ben's life! Save Ben's life!"

Alex's phone is already up, catching every second. Her smile is wide. "That'll play well on the feed."

Briggs rakes a hand through his hair. "Well . . . looks like I'm going to Miller's Crossing."

I raise my hand without hesitation. "I'm in."

Alex slips her phone into her bag and smooths her dark hair into place. "I'll sit this one out. I've got a massage at two." She flashes a grin. "But keep me in the loop—I'll catch up with you later."

Scout noses my palm like she can feel the storm building. I scratch her head, eyes already on Briggs. "Let's go get this warrant."

Briggs and I weave through the chanting crowd, Scout glued to my side. The protesters press in, shoving phones in our faces, but Briggs keeps his head down, bulldozing a path toward my Bronco. Scout seems reluctant to give up the front passenger seat, but Briggs offers her a doggie treat in exchange.

I flash a smile. "Do you always keep dog bones in your pocket?"

He laughs. "My dog loves them. I have a yellow lab too. Her name is Molly. We should let them play together sometime."

"For sure." My heart does a little pitter-patter. Is this a date—for more than our dogs?

I fall quiet, letting the thought roll around while the world blurs past my window. It's crazy how much my life has shifted. If you'd told me two weeks ago I'd be setting up dog playdates with none other than Lawson Briggs, I'd have laughed you off the dock.

We hit the highway, winding past soybean fields and patches of pine. I glance over as casually as I can manage. "So . . . you and Alex."

His head jerks toward me. "What about me and Alex?"

"You two looked pretty cozy back there. Little hand-on-the-chest action."

Color creeps up his neck. "She does that to everybody."

I smirk, letting him squirm a beat before softening. "Relax, Briggs. She's good at what she does. Just don't let her eat you alive."

He exhales through his nose, shaking his head. "You're impossible. She's like ten years older than me anyway."

"And if she wasn't?"

He shrugs. "She's not really my type." A beat of silence, then: "Why do you always call me Briggs? I have a first name, you know."

"Habit. That's what Tommy always called you." I laugh. "For the longest time, I thought Briggs *was* your first name."

The smile fades from his lips. "I remember," he says, his voice softer, rough around the edges.

For a second, I see it—the grief that still shadows him, the friend he lost, and the years that haven't dulled it.

His smile returns. "In that case, you have my permission to keep calling me Briggs."

Something tugs in my chest. "Deal," I say quietly, eyes on the road.

Several miles slip by in comfortable silence before I speak again. "Ben's awake. The doctor called me on the way to lunch. That's why I was late. To better protect Ben, I told Brody to keep it under wraps for now."

Briggs mutters a curse under his breath. "Then we'd better

move fast. If Clay catches wind, he won't hesitate to try again. I wish you'd told me sooner."

"I wasn't sure whether to trust Alex."

His jaw tightens. "You can trust her. But you're right—the fewer people who know, the better."

The brick courthouse in Miller's Crossing rises like a fortress against the sky, smaller than Tidewell's but somehow more welcoming. Judge Carmichael's clerk ushers us straight into chambers, no waiting, no stalling.

Carmichael is silver-haired, lean, and sharp-eyed. He flips through Briggs's affidavit, lips pressed in a line. The room is so still I can hear the ticking of the wall clock and Scout's soft huff at my feet.

Finally, Carmichael looks up. "I've been following this case. Your reasoning is compelling, and frankly, overdue. You'll have your warrant."

Relief washes over me like a tide breaking against the shore. My shoulders sag as the burden of these past weeks lifts—just enough to let me breathe again.

Briggs exhales, too, his pen scratching as he signs where directed. The judge stamps the last page with a crisp thud and slides it across the desk.

"Serve it swiftly and carefully," Carmichael says, his voice low but firm. "Men like Dalton don't go down easy."

I pick up the warrant, the weight settling heavy in my hands. "Don't worry, Your Honor. He won't slip through this time."

Minutes later, we're back on the road, Scout's head poking between the seats. Briggs glances at me, the ghost of a smile tugging at his mouth. "Do you have a plan, Detective? You heard what Carmichael said. Men like Dalton don't go down easy."

"I'm not afraid." I place a hand over my heart. "Addie's watching over me."

Chapter Thirty-Five

We're ten miles outside Tidewell when my phone buzzes on the console. *Brody.*

I press the speaker button. "Talk to me."

"Detective, someone tipped off Dalton. He knows about the warrant." Brody's voice is tight, breathless.

My fingers clamp around the wheel. "How do *you* know about the warrant, Brody?"

"I have a source on Carmichael's team. But I didn't tell anyone. I swear."

I force out a deep breath. I have no choice but to trust him. "Where are you?" I snap.

Brody's quivering voice fills the car. "Half a block down from his place—eyes on his driveway. He's hauling duffels into his truck like he's fixing to disappear. What do you want me to do?"

My pulse spikes. "Get units in position, but nobody moves until I give the order. If Dalton knows we're coming, we can't go charging in blind. Keep your car out of sight and your line open— I'm ten minutes out."

Briggs shoots me a wary look. "If he gets wheels under him, he'll head for the water. We'll lose him."

"Not if we cut him off first." I press harder on the gas. Scout whines softly from the backseat, picking up on the tension thrumming through the Bronco. "Hang on, girl. Hang on, Briggs. Clay Dalton's not slipping through my fingers. This ends today."

In the absence of blue flashing lights, I flip on my hazards and barrel down the last few miles at ninety.

As we approach Clay's street, I spot Brody's white Honda, but no units in sight.

"Where's the backup I ordered?" I slam the heel of my hand against the steering wheel. "They're blatantly disregarding my order. The whole damn department is Team Clay. We're on our own here, Briggs." I slam on the brakes. "Get out while you can."

He points at the road ahead. "Drive, Sutherlin. I'm not going anywhere."

I grit my teeth and keep going. Brody flashes me a thumbs-up as I drive by, signaling that Clay is still at home.

Clay is locking the back door when I screech into his driveway, cutting my Bronco sideways to block his truck. I kill the engine and jump out, badge raised. "Clay Dalton, you're under arrest—"

Clay freezes, eyes wide, like a deer caught in a hunter's sights. He appears unarmed—though he might have a gun tucked into the back of his waistband.

Scout launches from the Bronco, hackles high, teeth bared, barking as if she's been waiting for this exact second. I draw my pistol, finger indexed along the frame, and sprint after her.

Clay bolts at the sight of the vicious animal charging toward him, out for blood. He scrambles up the privacy fence, heaves himself over the top, and vanishes into the neighborhood beyond.

I find the gate, but it's locked from the inside. Far off, I catch sight of Clay, vaulting one backyard fence after another like a cornered fox.

I whistle to Scout. "Come on, girl—we'll cut him off at the pass."

As we blow past the Bronco, I shout to Briggs, "He's headed for the waterfront. Follow us—we're going on foot!"

Scout surges ahead, ears flat, a streak of muscle and fury. We tear down Tidewater Drive toward the waterfront shops, dodging cars and weaving through startled pedestrians. My lungs burn, but adrenaline keeps my legs pumping. Scout clears a planter, then vaults a bar table crowded with men and pints of beer. Glass shatters, curses erupt, but she lands clean and keeps going—locked on Clay's scent.

Once he clears the waterfront, Clay cuts across Route 22. I figure he's headed for a boat at Patriots Landing, but instead he guns a left onto the narrow access road—the one that leads past the Bayview dump, the same stretch where I found Scout all those mornings ago.

When he reaches the end of the road, he spins to face us, chest heaving, eyes wild.

I grab Scout's collar, fighting to hold her back. "I know, girl. I want the same thing. But killing him would be the easy way out. He needs to pay the slow way—behind bars."

Tires squeal behind me. My Bronco slides to a stop. I shout, "Grab the leash!"

Briggs is at my side in a second, clipping the leash to Scout's collar. He jerks the line taut and takes control. "Got her."

"I'm warning you, Sutherlin. Stay out of this." Clay's eyes flicker wild, panic lacing his threat. "You don't know who you're messing with."

"I've got a badge and a warrant." I wave the paper at him. "You're the one who should be afraid."

"You'll never get a conviction," he snarls. "You don't have the evidence."

When he digs a hand into his pocket, I raise the pistol, feet wide, body braced for impact. "Hands up, Clay. Don't make me shoot."

Slowly removing his hand, he holds a small object up to the sun. The light catches it, throwing a scatter of stars across the water.

My breath stops.

Clay's grandmother's diamond. Addie's engagement ring.

He flicks his wrist, and the ring spins end over end, dropping into the black water.

Everything happens at once. I lunge for the ring, and Scout explodes forward, the leash yanking from Brigg's hands with furious momentum. She snaps at Clay's ankle, teeth catching denim. Clay howls and stumbles back, losing his balance. I seize the opportunity—driving my shoulder into him and twisting his arm, slamming him face-first into the mud. I cuff his hands, the metal clicking shut around his wrists. Scout snarls over him, body low and triumphant.

Clay glares over his shoulder at me, water and mud spattering his face. "Lock me up all you want," he spits. "The Old Guard will bury you."

Briggs rights himself. "That sounds like a threat to me, Dalton." He kneels beside him, calm and deliberate. You're under arrest for the murder of Addie Dalton, threatening a law enforcement officer, and conspiracy to commit the murder of Ben Holloway."

I haul Clay to his feet and hand him off to Briggs, then wade into the shallows, hands plunging through the cold murk for the ring. But it's long gone—a silent marker at the bottom of the marsh for everything Addie lost.

I can't bring her back. I can't save the baby she never got to hold. But I can damn sure make Clay Dalton rots for what he did.

———

I hope *Dark Current Rising* found you at just the right moment and wrapped you in all the feels along the way.

Be on the lookout for the next two installments in The Sutherlin Files trilogy, *Dark Current* and *Dark Current Reckoning*.

If you're craving more emotional, character-driven stories set in the South, be sure to explore my other series, including Marsh Point, Sandy Island, and the Soul Seekers Collection.

Loved this book?

If this story touched you, would you consider leaving a quick review on Amazon?

Your support helps other readers find my books. Thank you from the bottom of my heart!

Acknowledgments

I'm forever indebted to the many people who help bring a project to fruition. My cover designer, the hardworking folks at Damonza.com. My beta readers: Alison Fauls, Anne Wolters, Laura Glenn, Lisa Hudson, Lori Walton, Rachel Story, Jaime Campanella, and Amy Connolley. Last, but certainly not least, are my select group of advanced readers who are diligent about sharing their advanced reviews prior to releases.

I'm blessed to have many supportive people in my life who offer the encouragement I need to continue my pursuit of writing. Love and thanks to my family—my mother, Joanne; my husband, Ted; and my amazing children, Cameron and Ned.

Most of all, I'm grateful to my wonderful readers for their love of women's fiction. I love hearing from you. Feel free to shoot me an email at ashleyhfarley@gmail.com or stop by my website at ashleyfarley.com for more information about my characters and upcoming releases. Don't forget to sign up for my newsletter. Your subscription will grant you exclusive content, sneak previews, and special giveaways.

* 9 7 8 1 9 5 6 6 8 4 8 8 9 *